# OBJECT OF

# YOUR LOVE

# OBJECT OF
# YOUR LOVE

## S T O R I E S

# DOROTHY
# SPEAK

*A Patrick Crean Book*

SOMERVILLE HOUSE PUBLISHING

TORONTO

**Canadian Cataloguing in Publication Data**

Speak, Dorothy
    Object of your love : stories

A Patrick Crean book.
ISBN 1-895897-72-6

I. Title.

PS8587.P24O35 1996    C813'.54    C96-931381-0
PR9199.3.S62O35 1996

Book design: Gordon Robertson
Cover photograph: Barbara Cole
Author photograph: Paul LaBarge

Printed in Canada

Published by Somerville House Publishing,
a division of Somerville House Books Limited,
3080 Yonge Street, Suite 5000, Toronto, Ontario M4N 3N1
Internet: SOMBOOKS@GOODMEDIA.COM
Web: HTTP://WWW.GOODMEDIA.COM/SOMERVILLEHOUSE

Somerville House Publishing acknowledges the financial assistance of the Ontario Publishing Centre, the Ontario Arts Council, the Ontario Development Corporation, and the Department of Communications.

*To Paul*

These stories (some in earlier forms and with
different titles) were previously published, as follows:

"Memorabilia," *University of Windsor Review*
"Object of Your Love," *Prism International*
    and *Journey Prize Anthology 1994*
"Summer Sky: White Ship," *New Quarterly*
"Eagle's Bride," *Northward Journal*
"Grass," *Grain*
"River Landscape," *A Room of One's Own*
"North of the Border," *Wascana Review*


*The author would like to thank the
Canada Council for financial assistance.*

# CONTENTS

# OBJECT OF YOUR LOVE

# E A G L E ' S
## B R I D E

*I am seized with violent desire*
*Alone by myself I become lustful.*
*I am seized with violent desire*
*Alone by myself I become lustful.*

– Inuit song

I LIVE with a married man on a hill overlooking an Arctic settlement. From the living-room window I can see the red roofs of fifty prefab houses (bungalows for the Inuit, two-stories for the whites) lining a muddy road curving around the shore, from the Catholic mission at one end to the RCMP station at the other. I can look out across the black hills ringing the bay, and beyond at the everlasting frozen sky. The first time I saw this landscape it made me shake. I thought I might have touched down on the fruitless crust of the moon, or the rocky, infertile road to Hell. Now I am in love with its beautiful desolation. There is a sense here that, like the land and the Inuit themselves, there are no beginnings or endings. There is only endurance.

I never met Ruth, Egan's wife. She left six months ago, just before I came to the community. And yet, I feel I know her. You cannot live day in and day out with someone's things and not know them. When I touch the Shaker dining-room chairs, or the antique decoy on the mantle, or the needlepoint cushions, I feel something that is not jealousy, though I have heard of women driven to homicidal thoughts from having to use another woman's dishes, towels, bed sheets. Sometimes I have to bite my tongue. Egan will not hear anything bad about Ruth, though he has consented to turn her photograph face down on the bureau. I like to think of her long, humourless face pressed hard against the walnut surface.

It is possible that I know Ruth better than I know Egan. He is an unreadable, angerless man, but I am not sure he was always this way. They say that any southerner who survives twenty years in the North, as Egan has, has either gone weird or was crazy to begin with. In the evenings, I see him with a book open on his knee, staring for hours at the crackling fire, feeding on his selfish grief like a hungry dog eating its own entrails. I have to get out then. I storm down the hill and stride back and forth on the road beside the bay, looking out at the black water. I walk rapidly, past curtainless windows flickering with blue television light, past houses where men and women sit at kitchen tables killing bottles of whisky.

When my legs ache so much that I can go no further, I climb back up the hill. I have to pass Ruth's greenhouse, perched twenty feet from the house on a cement pad. It is the greenhouse that convinced me that Ruth must have been, in the end, quite mad. She tried to grow lettuce, tomatoes, orchids—*orchids!*—but of course they died during the dark months. The greenhouse stands beside Egan's A-frame, on sunny days glittering like a prism above the community. "Ruth's Folly," I call it privately.

When Egan is away on business trips to the South, I have seen the raven-haired Inuit children creep up the hill like hunters, step inside the greenhouse, cautiously, superstitiously, gazing round in wonder at the patterns of frost on the windows, intricate as stained glass, at the transparent, soaring ceiling, glorious and divine as a

Gothic cathedral. I hear their voices echoing against the brittle walls like the thin cry of seagulls flown too far north or the sound of Ruth's ghost weeping. The children dump the earth out of Ruth's green plastic pots, dump it on the cement floor, and jubilantly bear the pots, like anthropologists' trophies, back down the hill. I have seen fragments of green plastic all over the community, lying in the dirt beside houses, or crushed underfoot on the pebbly beach. I've seen dogs chewing on them.

"Why don't you stop them if you see them doing it?" Egan has asked, smiling sadly, with the same tolerant, paternal expression he uses for the Inuit, and probably with his own children. (I am not much older than his daughter.)

"The greenhouse is preposterous. Why don't you have the silly thing pulled down?" I answer.

"I'm used to seeing it there."

"How can I replace," I demand angrily, "how can I *hope* to replace a woman who still lives all around me?"

I came North looking for freedom, a virgin country, a society where there were no rules. Almost immediately I was hired as book-keeper at the art cooperative, where prints are produced, raw stone sold to carvers, completed sculptures purchased back from them and marketed to the South. I was given the bachelor apartment above the co-op. It was small and poorly heated, with bare windows looking out at the relentless horizon. Like a nun entering her cell, I embraced its brutal simplicity. The cold pine floors and rigid sofa bed made me feel pure and strong. I thought I wanted to live an essential, bedrock existence—like the treeless landscape I saw from my window.

Several times, though, in the months after my arrival, I was forced to spend a few nights in Egan's spare bedroom. There is always a housing shortage in the community and, with Ruth and the children gone, he had more empty rooms than anyone else in the settlement. Being owned by the co-op, my apartment was often

3

given over to official visitors—art historians, photographers, government officials—curious about the richest art community in the North, a settlement where there is a Ski-Doo at every door and a TV antenna on every roof. With the snow driving hard against the windows of the A-frame, Egan fed me exotic foods: watermelon, fresh artichokes, cashew nuts, things the Inuit have never heard of or seen. He never shops at the local Hudson's Bay store, where everything is sold dry or frozen; he can afford to fly all his groceries in from Timmins. He has a microwave oven, a Cuisinart, a dishwasher, a VCR, a waterbed. There isn't a piece of furniture in his house that isn't a century old. If you were to close the living-room curtains and shut out the vista of thin islands of ice floating on the blue bay, you could believe you are sitting in an upper-middle-class Toronto home.

But even for a man like Egan, who has lived in the Arctic nearly as long as he can remember, there are moments when the vastness of the landscape, the penetrating cold, the sight of the cruel hills and the jarring peacock sky can rock you to your core. Loneliness sets in, followed swiftly by despair. One feels a need to cleave to another human body, like the Inuit babies that lived inside their mother's parkas, wearing nothing but a piece of caribou hide for a diaper, skin pressed against skin, the smells of their bodies intermingling. One evening, during a week-long sojourn with Egan, we climbed the stairs together to retire to our respective rooms. But then Egan turned to me on the little landing and said, his hand on the light switch of his room, "Will you sleep with me tonight?" I didn't need to be persuaded. I was already aroused by his melancholy and restlessness, by his square bristly jaw and frontiersman's shoulders.

Egan has turned out to be a methodical, conservative lover. I put this down to Ruth's passionlessness: it is from a woman that a man learns to make love. His caresses are sorrowful, weary, bordering on penitent. Our love-making seems for him a cautious physical pleasure, but it does not satisfy his soul. I have never been convinced

4

that he feels comfortable about what we are doing. But when I lie with my long thick hair thrown across the pillow and my bare breasts heaving, I do not see how he could prefer making love to plain Ruth. Sometimes, afterwards, he will lie very still beside me and I will turn to him in the dark, expecting to see his lips moving silently. I think he might be praying for Ruth to come back.

Under the house lives a white hare, which Egan feeds daily, squatting on his haunches, offering a carrot. The hare appeared the day Ruth left him. Egan sent word around the community that it was not to be hunted down and killed for someone's supper. I am convinced that Egan believes the hare is Ruth's spirit. That's why he's been throwing leafy vegetables under the house, to keep it alive. After half a lifetime up here, he may put some store in the Inuit notion that everything, animate and inanimate, has a spirit, an *inua*. He believes in transference. A person can become an animal, an animal a person. Creation is fluid. Physical manifestations are merely arbitrary boundaries, through which the soul can migrate, take up residence in another life form.

With Egan's money, Ruth has gone to live in an expensive suburb of Toronto, in a fortresslike stone house with a great medieval wooden door and dense boxwood shrubs clipped to look like unicorns and dragons. She has placed the children in private schools. At first she said Egan might be able to join her later, in the South. She thought that the smog and traffic noise, the long shadows cast by skyscrapers, the pace of city life would obscure the flaws in him that had become so painfully manifest in the pitiless northern light. But when he goes south, she will not let him stay in the house. When she sees him, she says, she feels the arctic wind blowing once more down her back. She is afraid that if she lets Egan near her, she will not be able to resist the strange spiritual pull of the North. Its wintry hand will come down on her, close around her throat.

Egan's children have become strangers to him. They wear the latest in labelled clothing, they go to a white school, they do not miss the North (the country of their birth!) or ever want to go back to it. When Egan visits Toronto, he rings the doorbell of Ruth's house and the children answer it. "Oh, Dad, it's you," they say coolly, in their new, sophisticated urban voices. "What are *you* doing here?" Until they moved south with their mother, he did not notice how much they resemble her. They have her hard, unforgiving mouth, her careful expressionlessness. Their faces are smooth and impervious as varnished wooden masks. Then Ruth will appear in the hallway behind them, her body rigid, her expression cold, cold as a soapstone carving, cold and distant as an iceberg floating on the Foxe Channel.

---

One afternoon at the cooperative, I open an invoice for ten bolts of duffle cloth that I can't remember ordering. That would be for the sewing project, I think. I take my cup of coffee and the invoice and set off to see Morgan. To reach the sewing studio, I must first pass through the stonecutting shop where three Inuit men are at work, transferring images on paper to the large stone blocks for the making of stonecut prints. These old men are very brown from a lifetime spent on a terrain offering not a sliver of shade from the raw arctic sun. They have shrunken necks, many missing teeth, bad haircuts revealing large flowery ears. Chipping silently away with chisels on the soft stone, they work without haste, smoking cigarettes. Their friends drop in to talk. This is allowed. We are lucky to get them to come in at all to do what they call "the white man's work." From time to time they get up and gaze longingly out the window at the land, their elbows, in threadbare sweaters, resting on the high windowsills. Their eyes narrow, scanning the horizon. They are watching for good hunting weather. If it comes, we may not see them again for weeks.

I find Morgan in the sewing room with four or five Inuit

women. They are using binder twine to tie up bunches of flowers, lichens and grass collected out in the rocky hills where they bloom, during a brief summer, in miraculous little pockets of blazing colour. These will be dried and then used to make natural dyes. The white duffle we import from the South will be stewed in great vats of colour, producing subtle burnt ochres, hazels, olives, saffrons. Then the women will cut up the cloth and sew Inuit fashions for the southern market, thick parkas with heavy whipstitch detail and appliqued seals, narwhal, bears, caribou, all the creatures that southerners want to believe still populate the North but which now in fact exist in abundance only in Inuit dreams.

When the Inuit women see me they become quiet and look down at their weathered hands. I respect these shy, tough, polite people. In their wise, passive eyes are reflected a history of death by starvation, intense cold, drowning on the sea-floe edge, a heritage of powerful legends involving giants, enchanted loons, man-eating monsters, the marriage of young women to eagles. But they are nervous around me because I am living with Egan. It is not that they pass judgement, as the whites do, but that Egan is their White God. He has run the art cooperative for two decades, buying their carvings and drawings, managing the marketing of their art. He is their lifeline to the bewildering South.

Some of these women may be bashful, too, because in the middle of the night they have come to Egan, who is the local justice of the peace. They climb the hill, bloody-faced, when their husbands have beaten them, and ask Egan what they should do. They come to him when their children have been caught by the RCMP, breaking into the nursing station for drugs or into the Hudson's Bay store for cases of Coca-Cola. Now they file past me out of the room, bowing and smiling to themselves. It is four thirty and time to go home. Some of the women wear large, expensive wristwatches, but do not consult them. Most of them were born in snowhouses, they know the precise time of day by the angle and quality of the light outside.

Morgan watches them go, saying, "*Tavvauvutit. Tavvauvutit.* Good night." She comes down from the ladder where she has been hanging the grasses and flowers from the ceiling to dry. She was the first friend I made here, but she became distant after I moved in with Egan. She and Ruth had been good friends.

"She used to sit up there and cry all day and wring her hands," Morgan said about Ruth after I had moved up the hill. When she told me this, tears ran down her sharp cheekbones and fell in a pot of ammonia and lichens that she was stirring on the stove in the sewing room.

"Is that my fault?" I asked angrily. "That she was unhappy here? I never met the woman."

The fact is this: Morgan was not grieving for Ruth, she was simply jealous that I was living with Egan. All the whites are envious that Egan and I have something fresh and passionate and unorthodox. They are trapped in their own dull framework of sin. They survive on gossip and liquor and isolation pay. They learn a little *Inuktitut* and exploit the Inuit, trading packs of cigarettes for valuable carvings, which they hope one day to sell to a museum for a fortune. They slip into traditional role-playing. While the women stay home baking and breast-feeding their babies, the men buy rifles and go hunting on weekends with the Inuit men, sliding smoothly over the snow in plywood boxes mounted on *komatiks* pulled by Ski-Doos. In the dark months of winter, when boredom and hysteria run high, the white men molest the Inuit daughters. Some go insane up here. They develop agoraphobia and must be carried blindfolded on stretchers across the airstrip to a waiting Twin Otter.

To avoid such a fate, Morgan married an Inuk, an older man who was once a powerful camp leader when these people lived on the land. She has produced six flat-faced children, each of them cursed with her frizzy fawn hair. She has become more native than the Inuit themselves, carrying her babies everywhere in the deep hood of an *amautik*, while the young Inuit mothers these days wear ordinary parkas purchased at the Hudson's Bay store and transport their children in their arms. She eats whale blubber and is a champion bannock maker, but to the Inuit she is still an outsider. Behind her back, they call her *Pinguarti*. "The Pretender." She claims that she is not white any more but, like other whites here, who live in a spiritual void, she turns her television set on for company when she gets up in the morning and leaves it going all day with the volume turned off, its images flickering like blue lightning across her living room, even when she's out of the house.

"Would you take a look at this invoice?" I ask her. "I can't find the order in my records."

She washes her hands slowly at the sink. I am sure she feels me watching her impatiently. She turns, pulling a towel from a rod on the wall, her habitually serious face spread thick with satisfaction. I can hear the whistle of her baby sleeping heavily in the hood of her *amautik*.

"What's the matter?" I say, dropping the invoice at my side.

Morgan dries her hands, watching my face carefully. "Ruth's coming back," she says with quiet triumph. I see the corners of her mouth twitch.

I stare at her for a moment, snort involuntarily, shake my head, look out the window and see snowflakes falling, as big as quarters. I believe for a moment that I must be hallucinating. I did not know we were due for a snowfall. Is it possible that I have fallen asleep at my ledger, that this is all a dream?

"I don't believe you," I say, and Morgan raises her eyebrows so confidently that my heart flies up in my throat and I ask, "When?"

"Tomorrow. On the morning flight."

"I thought she hated it here," I say.

"The city gave her claustrophobia," Morgan tells me. "She thought the skyscrapers were going to fall on her head."

I go looking for Egan but I don't find him in his office. His jacket is gone from its hook. He must be home, starting dinner. I burst out the side door of the cooperative, forgetting my own coat, leap down the wooden steps and head up the hill at a half-run. The wet snowflakes hit me in the face, and in the open neck of my shirt, but I don't shiver. I'm sweating with anger. The muddy road has frozen during the afternoon.

The snow is falling so thick that I can barely make out the A-frame as I turn off the road. They tell me that at the height of winter up here the skin freezes after thirty seconds out of doors. Moisture crystallizes in the lungs, it is painful to breathe. The sun shines briefly, white and cold in the sky. I had looked forward to deep winter and coming inside with frostbitten patches like white kisses on my face. I had pictured Egan rubbing my cheeks with his great thick hands until my skin burned. The air is dense with spinning snowflakes. I think of Ruth arriving out of the hot, brilliant, windy southern autumn to this gift, this miracle of snow in September. I think of her living the winter that was supposed to have been mine.

I stamp the snow off my boots, my hand is on the doorknob and I am about to enter the house. Then I notice Egan ten yards away, looking under the house. When I go and stand over him, he straightens up and looks at me calmly. He is a man who is not conscious of how attractive he really is. I look at his ruddy face and his even white teeth, thinking he would make a perfect advertisement for the hardy arctic life. He wears mountain boots and thick cable sweaters and, now that the weather is colder, a navy mariner's wool cap pulled down to his greying eyebrows. He searches my face to see if I've heard the news.

"Ruth is coming back," I say, hoping it isn't true, inviting him to deny it. He might still stop her if he wanted to. A phone call could prevent her from boarding the plane.

"And the hare is gone," he answers, as though completing a riddle. His gestures seem to me lighter, more optimistic than I have ever known them, his face, at fifty, suddenly serene and youthful. I see that, all along, what I have taken in him for grief was in fact patience. I wonder this: all those evenings when Egan was moving on top of me, slowly, deliberately, like a great hairy musk-ox swaying out on the tundra, was he holding, in his mind, the image of Ruth's adamant face, her unimaginative, biscuit-coloured hair falling in a dull curve? Or worse—and this is a notion I can scarcely bear—was he in fact employing me as bait, as a kind of cheap decoy, to lure a jealous Ruth back to him? Is this possible? Did he send her subtle and indirect messages, possibly enlisting Morgan as an unwitting but able agent—for surely she has been in touch with Ruth all along, surely the moment I crossed Egan's threshold, her brittle air-mail letters were winging their poisonous way southward, shooting, fragile as breath, above the snowy craters to fall through the brass letter slot of Ruth's massive oak door.

"Did you ever," I ask him pitiably, "did you ever love me? Or were you thinking always about Ruth?"

Egan does not answer my question. Perhaps he cannot. He moves on quickly to practicalities. "The wisest thing for you to do now is to leave the community," he tells me. "The sooner the better. There's a good chance you could get out in the morning." I see that he wants to spare Ruth the embarrassment of meeting me on the road. He wants to erase overnight what we had, to restore the past. How convenient for him if I were to board the very flight from which Ruth alights in the morning, take the seat warmed by her body on her way north, while the plane lifts, banks, turns its nose toward the equator, carrying me away forever. The very thought of it rankles me.

"Why should I go?" I ask bitterly. "Why should I leave a place I love, just for your comfort?"

"Stella," he says kindly, taking a step forward, reaching out to touch my arm, but I pull away. "Don't do this to yourself," he tells me. "You're young. You have a long life ahead of you. Get out now while you can. Escape this godforsaken place."

"Don't talk down to me," I say angrily. "I'm not a child. I've been your lover!" I look away, my eyes falling on Ruth's greenhouse, which stands darkly against the luminous sky. Perhaps I should not have scoffed at the glass house. Perhaps it is not Ruth's Folly, after all, but Ruth's Triumph, her private monument, fragile defiance of this infertile land, this bald and windswept curve of the earth with its strange power to seduce, absorb, unite.

Then, contradicting myself, I do something that is just like what one of Egan's spoiled children might do. I pick up a ski pole that has been leaning against the house all summer. Stepping toward the greenhouse, I raise the pole high, feeling the need, the right, to smash something. I bring it down on the greenhouse wall, connect with the glass, feel it shattering beneath my blow. Again I raise the pole and bring it down. I am hot and trembling with sweet revenge, expecting that, at any moment, Egan will step forward and grab me, pin my wrists against my sides. Perhaps this is what I want. Perhaps I long to feel one last time his iron grip, the power he has over me, over this community. But he stays where he is, willing, it would seem, to let me do whatever damage I want, if it will satisfy me, get me out of his life. I continue my destruction, wielding the pole like a sword, cleaving the air with it. Slivers of glass fly like rain. I feel them piercing the backs of my hands like needle pricks. When Ruth arrives in the morning, I think, when she climbs up the hill, she will find in ruins whatever hopes or illusions the greenhouse embodies for her. I swing the pole. The splintering of glass, like brittle thunder, will be heard, I believe, down in the settlement. I hope it will carry over the round hills and clear out across the icy bay.

I walk down the road in darkness to the co-op building. I have never officially given up my apartment above the print shop. It has not been assigned to anyone else. I intend to reoccupy it. I fish for the key I am sure must be somewhere at the bottom of my purse, open a side door, climb the narrow stairs. Unready to face the heartlessness of the rooms, the unadorned walls, the mean furniture, the cold, textureless surfaces, I do not turn on the lights, but rest in darkness at the kitchen table with my coat on.

The image comes to me of Egan climbing the stairs of the A-frame, changing the bed sheets, moving about the room looking for anything I might have left behind: a comb, a pocket novel, a letter. I picture him stepping to the bureau, setting upright once more the photograph of Ruth, whose face has been thrust for so long against the bitter wood. The Resurrection of Ruth. Her picture gazes now upon the room, upon the bed where Egan and I made love, repossessing them. I do not sleep that night. Just after dawn, I hear the distant drone of a Twin Otter. Moving to the window, still in my coat, for I have not even turned on the heat in the apartment, I see the plane grow large and dark in the sky, making its approach to the airstrip, circling above the community, banking neatly, its wings catching the unobstructed rays of the rising sun.

———————

Egan will no longer employ me at the co-op. My presence there would be awkward, now that Ruth has returned. However, he does not have the nerve to expel me from the apartment. A wise and patient man, he may believe that time will eventually drive me out. I manage to get a job almost immediately at the Hudson's Bay store, doing the books. The store is on the far edge of the community, at the end of the road that hugs the bay, among hills of empty oil drums thrown out in the snow to rust. Here, exiled from the co-op, at the distant perimeter of the settlement, I sit in a small, dim office at the back, with a window looking out into the store. I can see the Inuit women listlessly pushing their carts up and down the bright, barren aisles. The Hudson's Bay store is, like the shopping malls of the South, an end in itself, a destination, a place to kill time. In the vacant afternoons, when snow falls steadily outside like an opaque white screen, the women drift in, they shuffle aimlessly through the store, staring at the shelves, searching, searching for something that will make them happy.

It is October now and we have many feet of snow. The Ski-Doos have come out and, at noon when I walk home for lunch, the teenaged boys are roaring up and down the narrow, high-banked, snow-packed roads, just as southern youth do in their hot rods on steamy summer nights. For my lunch, I heat canned soup on my hot plate and butter a slice of bread, thinking sometimes of the imported green grapes Egan used to feed me, one by one, his great square fingers lingering in my mouth like succulent fruit.

Each day now, looking down out of my window, I see Ruth emerge from one of the cooperative buildings, cross the road and enter another door. She is shorter and slighter than I expected, slender-hipped as a girl and dressed in flat laced shoes, conservative plaid skirts and simple sweater sets. She carries in her arms an archival box full of drawings, bears it high, like a priestess transporting a sacred offering, stepping sure-footedly through the snow. I can see from the rigid set of her shoulders, from her efficiency and brusqueness, that there is a hard knot within her, that she is all turned inward upon herself.

I have never been introduced to her, but one day, late in September, we came upon each other on the road, or rather, she stopped me when she could conveniently have passed by. I'd been looking the other way, distracted. But she pressed forward, caught my arm. She had evidently been waiting for the moment when we would come face to face, perhaps she had even set out to hunt me down. She seemed to have composed something to say.

"I know who you are," she told me quietly, confidently, "and why you are still here. You are not important to me. You don't matter to me in any way. Do you understand? You are not a threat. This is something you should know." All I could do was to stare at the unhappy lines chiselled around her mouth. I wanted to believe that she was lying to herself, to me, but I could not. I saw that she was rock hard, impermeable as the land, with a centre like flint, like the stony hills pressing in on us.

Down at the store, I have heard that Ruth has ordered new plastic pots for her greenhouse, she has ordered new panes of glass. When they arrive an Inuk will have to toil for days out in the cold with putty and knife to repair the damage of a jealous mistress. The greenhouse will be restored to its former majesty. It will again be like a soaring medieval cathedral and Ruth will be its high priestess. She will be productive again. She will have, beneath her fingernails, rich, pungent imported soil flown in alongside her filets mignons and avocado pears. Once more she will grow salad greens. When Egan comes home from work he will find her fragile orchids quivering in a vase on the maple hall table.

The evenings seem interminable in my little apartment. I do not look very closely at my surroundings for fear they will make me desire the warmth and comforts of Egan's home. I have stayed in the apartment, though I no longer find its poverty cleansing. There is no other place for me to live and I was right in thinking that Egan would not expel me. He does not want to turn our quarrel into a public drama, though, technically, the apartment is for the housing of cooperative staff. After work I eat dinner alone, watch television, read books. Late at night I lie in bed, listening to the crunch of footsteps on dry snow, to voices passing below on the road.

The bay is frozen now, the ice is a foot thick. On Saturday mornings I hear a great roaring of Ski-Doo engines down on the shore. Stepping to my window, I see a group of hunters heading out across the bay, rifles glinting in their laps, striking out in search of the seal pods at the distant floe edge. The runners of the long *komatik* sleds leave clean parallel lines on the untracked snow. Gradually, the drone of the Ski-Doos dies away, the figures of the hunters, dark against the dazzling white landscape, diminish, finally disappearing between two hills sloping down to the mouth of the harbour.

Sometimes as I move about my apartment on the weekends I

hear commotion in the rooms downstairs. It is November and a new collection of graphics is about to be released to the southern market. There is a great flurry of activity. Thirty images in editions of fifty must be hand-printed, orders packed up and shipped. All day long, the sound of voices, heavy feet falling on the crude wooden floors, the scraping of furniture legs, the ring of hammers striking nails into wooden crates rise to where I sit with my hands wrapped around a hot cup of tea. One Sunday evening late in the month, when all the commotion downstairs has subsided, I hear a quiet knock at my door. It is the first caller I've had since moving back to the apartment. I think at first that it must be Egan. I realize I have been praying all these months for his defection from Ruth, never believing he wanted her back. Flushed and trembling with gratitude, I rush excitedly to the door and open it. However, standing on the little landing is not Egan, but Moses Akulukjuk, the young co-op manager, a smile, alternately bold and sheepish, flitting across his face. Endeavouring to conceal my disappointment, I invite him in.

"It is not the same without you at the co-op, Stella," he says sadly, shaking his head. "Mr. Egan. He should not fire you." He slips out of his boots and jacket, looks around curiously at the apartment, pads in heavy wool socks to my kitchen table. I reach down another mug from the cupboard but I know already that Moses has not come here for tea. I sit down opposite him, reflecting to myself that winter is upon us and my bed is cold.

We become lovers. In the following weeks he slips up to my apartment under cover of darkness. It is a bitterly cold December, a month when a white sun, pale and dull as the moon, rises at eleven in the morning, hangs low on the horizon for three hours, then drops from view. In this brief silver light, the landscape is alien and haunting. One must burn one's electric lights all day long.

When Moses arrives in the evenings, brazenly entering my apartment without knocking, I am ready for him. I have opened up the sofa bed, turned back the covers. He is small and slight, a good foot shorter than I, but his zeal more than compensates for his diminutive stature. He makes love swiftly, unabashedly, licking and grunting, probing, clambering greedily over my body like a bold little animal sniffing out a rich landscape. His great-great-great-grandfather was a white whaler, but the intervening years have erased any traces of his white ancestry. I find his coffee-brown skin, his wide flat face, his hairless chest enticing. Burying my fingers in his glossy black hair, I call him "My Little Wolf." Moses strokes my white thighs and says that they remind him of the smooth, flawless ivory he sells to the carvers for their sculptures. He teaches me some *Inuktitut* vocabulary. I ask him to tell me all the *Inuktitut* words for obscenities. He laughs, a little puzzled, but complies.

"Stella," he says, "you are maybe a little crazy?"

He was born in one of these prefab houses. He doesn't know how to hunt or make an igloo. He learned his English from comic books. He asks me if I will take him to Toronto for a holiday. He would like to see the view from the CN Tower. He has heard of Wonderland. He has three young children and a wife who drinks too much. Everyone in the community knows they are not happy. Nevertheless, I send him home at midnight, for the sake of appearances. Standing at my window, watching him walk away in the moonlight, I think that it is a bit of a coup for Moses to be bedding me now. He is a young, clever, ambitious man who would like to have Egan's job. There is a movement germinating in the community for greater independence, talk of getting rid of the white resource staff. Some day, in the near or distant future, Moses may replace Egan, the White God. In the meantime, he will sleep with Egan's ex-lover. And am I too, I wonder, am I using this affair as a way of striking back at Egan, of undermining his dangerous power here, of mocking him?

Despite my precautions, our love affair is no secret in the community. There is no such thing as privacy in a place this size. The sound of footsteps on the snowy road, the opening and closing of doors bring faces to every window. Gossip is endemic here, it poisons conversation. On my way to work, the Inuit nod to me, then pass on, smiling their secretive, comprehending smiles. This is the maddening thing about them: they see straight through everything. They are a people who, in order to survive, had to be able to stand in a stormy landscape which, from sky to earth, was like a great, dazzling white curve, like the featureless inside of an egg, and find their way, detect invisible landmarks, locate their buried cache of food beneath smooth snowdrifts, or die. When they see me in the road, they smile not out of mockery but out of amazement at the folly of people. For generations, they have witnessed the profound indiscretion of human beings, leading to murder, starvation, madness out on the unyielding land where nothing can be hidden.

---

One Sunday afternoon in April, I meet Morgan on the road outside the cooperative. I am carrying my skis and poles, warmly dressed for a few hours of cross-country skiing. It is some months since I have seen her.

"You're pregnant again," I say, because I notice that she is pale, her face gaunt. She laughs sadly. Her coat is open to the wind. She is wearing an old sweater stained from the spitting up of her young children. I smell thick, sweet liquor on her breath.

"How many months?" I ask her.

"Only two," she says, "but, as usual, I'm sick as a dog." She is a robust, heavy-hipped woman but her body does not bear children well. The process seems alien, hostile to her very nature. She has told me she always loses weight at the beginning of her pregnancies. She vomits and suffers from depression. Her husband, Manasie, whose own frame has been tempered by arctic winds, by sub-zero temperatures, whose torso, at seventy, is still sound, obdurate as the terrain, says this depression is a white weakness, a southern luxury. She is his fourth wife, the other three having died in childbirth out on the land, the blocks of a snowhouse roof curving over their heads, or of tuberculosis here in the community clinic. He will not let Morgan use birth control. He wants a large family. He wants many sons, the hunters of the future.

Morgan draws from her coat pocket a mickey of whisky, unscrews the top, holds the bottle out to me. I see the veins standing out like blue roots on the backs of her hands.

"No, thanks," I say. "I have to be going. I want to catch the best of the sun."

She shrugs and takes a drink herself. "We should get together again," she says, watching me as she drops the bottle back in her pocket. "For a drink or something."

"Yes," I say without conviction. I head off. On the edge of the community, I snap on my skis and glide over dry, powdery snow into the hills. I try to picture Morgan arriving in the community as a young woman, ten years ago, bringing with her a diploma in fashion design and a ruthless determination. I reflect that the North seems to attract these hard-edge types like a lodestone, metal to metal, people fleeing the ghosts and failures of their past, running from themselves as they cross the treeline and head toward the Arctic Circle, brash, fearing nothing but their own emptiness. I wonder if Morgan thought when she arrived here that, at thirty, she'd be bearing her seventh child. She once told me she'd married Manasie because he was harder, stronger than she. "He was a leader," she said, "and I'd got tired of leading."

In the middle of the afternoon, I am skiing on a ridge a few kilometres from the settlement. I pause, wanting to appreciate the panorama, the impressive sweep of the land, the pearly moisture frozen like crystals in the air. I have not seen a soul all afternoon but now, into my vision, slide two figures, also on skis, cutting across a slope a hundred feet below me. It is Egan and Ruth. Without noticing me, they too stop, draw something from their backpacks, perhaps thermoses of tea, exchange a few words, store away their thermoses, pick up their poles. I watch them move away. Soon Egan is skiing well ahead of Ruth, it is a struggle for her to keep up. She moves slowly, without energy or zeal. I have heard that Egan has been away a lot lately. He must fly to Toronto, New York, San Francisco to promote the community's art, leaving Ruth here.

I have passed Egan's house at night, seen a single light burning in a single room and wondered what Ruth does with her time. I have heard she is an accomplished knitter. She makes me think of the legend of the Eagle's Bride: a young Inuit woman picked up by an eagle and flown to a high sea cliff, where she is imprisoned in a nest and must bear the eagle's human-bird children. The girl asks the eagle to bring her a whole young caribou so that, when he is out hunting, she can braid the caribou sinew into a long line for her escape. I think of Ruth alone at night knitting a strong wool rope that stretches through all the rooms and doorways of Egan's house, seeking deliverance. Hasn't she merely, I think, exchanged one kind of suffocation for another: urban skyscrapers for these encroaching hills? Now the figures of Egan and Ruth disappear behind a ridge. I look around at the landscape and marvel at the power of such vastness to crush one.

---

A few weeks later, I come home for lunch and find a pair of hiking boots on my landing. Cautiously, I enter the apartment and see Morgan lying on my sofa. She turns, her face flushed, and looks at me.

"I wasn't feeling well," she says. "I came here. I'm sorry. I couldn't think of any other place. I remembered there was an extra key to your apartment in Egan's desk drawer. I had nowhere else to go." Her legs are pressed up against her belly. I touch her forehead.

"You're burning up," I say.

She tells me that several days ago she aborted her baby using a knitting needle. She told no one. The abortion itself went well but now some kind of infection seems to have set in. She is weak and inert with pain.

"I can't go home," she tells me. "Manasie will suspect something. What should I do?"

I sit down at the kitchen table. "You need to see the nurse," I say.

"I can't go to the clinic," she says firmly. "They'll find out what I've done. Everyone will know. Manasie will be disgraced. He'll want to get rid of me. He'll take another wife."

"Why haven't you gone to Ruth for help, instead of me?" I ask, thinking she has a nerve, coming here.

She pauses, her face full of disappointment. "Ruth has changed," she says, "since she went south. She's become distant. I'm not sure where her loyalties lie now. I don't want to take a chance of things leaking out. Whereas you . . ." she paused. She was going to say, *whereas you have no friends here.* "There must be some way you can get medication for me, some roundabout way," she goes on. "You could go to the clinic and pretend to be sick. Say you have an ear infection. Anything to get ahold of some antibiotics."

I say I don't see how I could do that, I have no fever, no symptoms of anything that could pass for infection. I feel angry that, with all her connections in the community, she's come to me, an outcast, someone she would not invite to her own home. I'm not willing to lie for her. Nobody here has ever lied to benefit *me.* I give her some aspirin, cover her with a blanket, put a cold cloth on her forehead.

"I have to get back to work," I say. Putting on my coat, I pause in the doorway and try once more. "Let me take you over to the clinic on my way," I say.

"I'm in too much pain to walk."

"Then let me get them to bring a stretcher over."

She closes her eyes and shakes her head. "I'll just sleep for a few hours and then see how I feel."

I am too busy at the store that afternoon to even think about Morgan, but I do book off early and hurry home. The apartment has grown dim and Morgan appears to be asleep. I turn on a light.

"Morgan?" I say, stepping forward, but she doesn't stir. The flush is gone from her cheeks. She is in fact grey. I reach out to touch her forehead, find it cold as a soapstone carving, and I know that she is dead. Sitting down on the edge of the couch, I stay there for some time, holding on to her lifeless hand, full of amazement at my own anger that afternoon, at the bitterness that had kept me from helping her. Feeling her fingers, light as twigs in my hand, I begin to shake because I know that I have become someone very different from the young woman who only a year ago first looked out these apartment windows.

An hour later one of the RCMP officers is sitting with me at my kitchen table taking notes. There will have to be an investigation into Morgan's death, he tells me. The coroner has been called and will fly in the next day. Now, some men come up from the co-op, wrap Morgan in a blanket and carry her out, struggling with her body down the narrow stairway. Moses is among them. He will not look at me. He acts like he's never been in the apartment before. Downstairs in the sewing room, Morgan's employees sit in a circle until well after six o'clock, there being no one there to tell them they can go home.

After the men are gone, the officer observes my pallor, my trembling hands. Even though the community is officially dry, even though the RCMP meet the weekly flight in the hope of apprehending liquor runners, he says to me, "You might want to have a good stiff drink," and I think of Morgan and her bottle of whisky. I tell the officer only that Morgan had been feverish and not strong enough to walk home and get into bed. I don't mention the abortion. Let them do their own digging, I think.

While the officer questions me, I listen for Egan's footsteps on the stair, wait to see his broad shoulders darkening the door. Given that he is justice of the peace, given Morgan's old friendship with Ruth, one might naturally expect him to take an interest. Also, I think, it would be a nice gesture for him to show me a little support, after what I've been through, but he does not come. Then the officer leaves and I am alone. Only now do I pour myself a drink. I have my pride, after all. I sit at the table, steadying my hands on the glass of scotch, disturbed, shocked not by Morgan's death but by my inability to be moved by it. I find I cannot feel sorrow or any kind of emotion for her and I realize that something within me too is dead, that it perished months ago.

As it turns out, Morgan died not of a botched abortion but of a burst appendix. The coroner reports that it had been ruptured for several hours, that the poisoning was well advanced by the time Morgan reached my apartment at noon. She would not have recovered in the clinic.

I attend her funeral, sitting in the back pew of the little white church. People do not want to look in my direction. They have no secret smiles left to give me. They wonder, I am sure, why Morgan had to die in my apartment, rather than in the clinic or at home, why I left her to die alone. They understand, it would seem, about the appendicitis, but they see me as some kind of accomplice in her death, an agent of bad luck. After the service is over, people stand around outside in the icy wind, watching as her coffin is carried to a shed behind the church, where it will be locked up until summer and the earth can be dug.

Seeing Moses on the edge of the crowd, I move to his side. In the three days since Morgan's death, I have not heard from him. "Come up tonight after work," I say to him quietly. "Please. I need you."

He shakes his head and looks away. "I cannot," he says. "It is not good. It is bad luck to lie there now." He looks small and cold in his parka, out here in the wind. I smile sadly at him, for I do not believe that he is superstitious. He is rejecting me because I have become too great a liability.

————————

A few weeks later, the Hudson's Bay store manager stops me on my way out to lunch and asks me to drop off a package for him at the airstrip. There is to be an unscheduled flight that afternoon at three o'clock and he wants the parcel to go with it. I carry it through town. It is mid-May and still there are no signs of spring here. The skies are dark and snow falls heavily, large wet flakes that coat your clothes. I wonder how long it will be before there is a thaw and Morgan can be properly buried. I wonder if she sensed, while she lay on my sofa, that she was dying, if she embraced the opportunity as the best way out, her only escape from Manasie, from the community.

I walk up the hill toward the airstrip. On my way past the cooperative, I pause, because I see Ruth sitting in the brightly lit archives building. Every morning she comes down from the house to catalogue drawings. This has been her job for at least a decade. During her brief absence in Toronto, Egan locked the door of the archives. No one was allowed to go in there. Now Ruth sits alone, day after day, at a large table, making her little pencil notations on the drawings, photographing them, storing them in expensive, airless, dust-free solander boxes, between sheets of acid-free tissue. There are tens of thousands of these drawings, stacks and stacks of them, dry and brittle and sometimes disintegrating, and more of them acquired every day. There is enough work there to last several lifetimes. Ruth can sit in this bright room until she is an old and addled woman and she will never be finished her work. The Eagle's Bride toiling away at her lonely task.

Observing her there, so fragile and solitary, the crude overhead light falling harshly on her lustreless hair, I remember her words to me that day on the road. *You are not important to me. You are not a*

24

*threat. This is something you should know.* For the first time, I wonder: Was there a hidden message there? A veiled kindness? Was she, I speculate, trying to help, rather than intimidate me? Was she saying that, if my intent in staying in the community was to punish her, it was only myself I would end up destroying? *This is something you should know.* While I had thought Egan was the strong one, I see now that it was always Ruth who was the pillar, the force, the magnet toward which Egan would soon be winging his way home, and without which he could never have survived this arctic hinterland. She is his marker, as indigenous to him as the stone *inukshuks* constructed out on the land by the Inuit to guide them through a featureless landscape.

Up on the airstrip, I enter the small, overheated office and push the package across the counter to the clerk. As I walk away, an idea occurs to me. "Is there room for passengers on the unscheduled flight?" I ask, turning back to the clerk. He consults a list on the counter, tells me they can probably fit me on.

At three o'clock I am seated in a Twin Otter, its sole passenger, with my back pressed against a wall of cargo. The flight will drop off freight in three other Baffin Island communities before it turns south again toward Timmins. From there I will catch a plane to Toronto. At my knee rests a single suitcase, in which I have packed a few clothes, leaving behind everything I acquired here in the past year. The throb of the engines fills my ears as the plane taxis down the short runway and takes off. I feel my spirits lifting unexpectedly with it, climbing. We bank, circle, pass above the community. I look out the window, down at the collection of tiny houses scattered across the terrain. From this height, they seem less a community than a random collection of vessels dangerously adrift in a white sea. Once again the plane tilts and, just before the settlement disappears from view, Ruth's greenhouse catches the sun's rays, flashing up at me, a brilliant and transitory fire in the cold snow, blinking its isolated message.

# A RIVER LANDSCAPE

FOR A LONG TIME, the only days the twins could remember were the good ones, when they came home after school to the crooked wooden house with its red front door and found all the lights on and fresh air blowing in through the back windows, which opened onto the river. They lived in a tiny, self-contained neighbourhood, a dozen or so streets cut off from the rest of the city by the river on one side and a large official estate on the other. On their own street, the houses, some in stone, some clapboard, all built around 1900, had been professionally renovated, with authentic trim and spindle rails and weathervanes and paint in gentle tones of ash or sulphur or leaf-green. And if their own narrow white house, with its overgrown garden, sagging porch, damaged gable and musty decay seemed shabby next to these, it was because their mother, Hedda, knew that all the beauty in the house was what time had wrought, that age had given it its depth and wisdom and character.

On those good days, the boys went down the narrow hallway to the back of the house and found Hedda wearing an old work shirt with the sleeves rolled up, sitting in the kitchen at the maple table with her great potter's hands—dried clay under her fingernails— laced around a mug of coffee, the old arthritic sheepdog, Charles, sleeping at her feet. The light, reflecting off the river, was tangible, miraculous, spiritual, and sometimes the twins thought that Hedda was its source, that everything flowed from her, the sunshine flooding across the scarred floorboards, the warmth of the kitchen, the vast expanse of maple table, the herbs growing on the windowsill, even the air they breathed: all of this originated with her, their lives would have had no texture, they would not have had a world to live in at all if Hedda had not created it for them. It seemed to Angus and Garreth that Hedda had even arranged for the slow grey river to flow behind the house and for a row of ancient willows, their twisted trunks big around as silos, to hang into the water like old women letting down their tangled hair.

No one else they knew could come home to this smell of fresh clay and oil paints, and their mother waiting always with something new to show them, one of her brilliant, wickedly clever clay scenes of seaside towns or villagescapes. Or, if she'd been out scavenging, found objects: an old wedding dress, a Niagara Falls cushion, a diary written in 1876, yellowed postcards, letters written by strangers, secondhand clothes, in the pockets of which they might discover handwritten notes, lucky rabbits' feet, coins, photographs, handkerchiefs. It seemed that Hedda brought the whole world into the house and together they would sit down and wonder what kind of persons might have once owned these things. Then their father would come in, and sometimes Hedda's dealer, Joseph, and though she was a small woman with a long lean face and something vulnerable in her pale grey eyes, they all drew strength from her and knew that none of them would be there at all if it weren't for Hedda.

But there comes a time in children's lives when they must begin to remember, and one April afternoon the boys came through the front door, two twelve-year-olds slender and light of limb and fresh-faced and susceptible. They saw Hedda hurtling down the hall toward them, her eyes crazy. She pushed past and out into the sunny day, where any sane person would be rejoicing at the sight of the crocuses thrusting through the grass and the tender leaves unfolding like tongues on the trees. Out on the driveway, Hedda pounded her head against the roof of the Datsun. Frozen on the porch, the boys watched but could not move toward her because she had become a stranger. Her long curly hair twisted, a wild bush in the wind. Finally, a neighbour ran out of a nearby house, pulled Hedda away from the car, pinned her arms back, gently pressed her down onto the damp earth. Surely there had been scenes before this, perhaps ones that Dempster had skilfully hidden from their knowledge or somehow smoothed over, but the boys could not remember them. That evening before dinner they watched Dempster pull the covers up over Hedda's shoulders, they glimpsed through the open bedroom door the welt rising like an eggplant on her forehead.

"Why did she do it, Dad?" they asked, their faces so knitted with injury and fear that he almost could not answer.

"Sometimes . . . sometimes your mother is overcome by . . . by powerful emotions she can't control. Don't worry about her. She's going to be all right. We're all going to be all right."

And so began the twins' acquaintance with Hedda's illness.

The days they dreaded—and this was often during the driving rains of fall—were when they came home and found the house dark after school and the mail still uncollected in the wicker basket hanging on the porch post. They listened anxiously in the front hall, holding their breath, their wet sneakers leaking onto the wide floorboards. Behind them the door stood open and a cold rain bounced off the street pavement. They saw shards of clay littering the hall, the cellar stairs. In the glass room off the kitchen they found Charles hiding in the fluff behind the old threadbare sofa Hedda had bought at the Salvation Army depot.

"Aw, shit, not again!" Garreth, now a tall, dark, lean-jawed teenager, spat out. He threw his backpack down on the floor. Angus, who in contrast was short, with his father's sandy colouring and soft teddy-bear shape, said, "We better check on her."

"Be my guest," said Garreth with disgust, heading for the kitchen.

"I'm getting something to eat." He was the older of the twins (older by about ten minutes) and the most impatient. As a baby, he'd screamed with colic until Hedda had wanted to drown him in the river. Angus, on the other hand, had been a docile infant, easy to please. Hedda's instinct, as a young mother of twins, had always been to pick up Angus first. Garreth sensed, even now, that she preferred Angus's company.

Then, while Angus climbed the stairs to look for Hedda, Garreth slipped into the powder room off the kitchen and quietly threw up.

Upstairs, Angus walked softly down the dark hallway, past what they all jokingly called "the storage room" (everything Hedda couldn't face—parking tickets, letters from her mother, bad reviews of her work, photographs of when she was young and, it would seem, happy—got thrown in there) and on to his parents' bedroom door. Opening it cautiously, he went in. By the ivory light falling through the window, he was able to make out the figure of Hedda in bed, her long brow and nose, her large lips and sunken chin, giving her the sad, passive profile of a ewe.

"Mom?"

Crossing the room, Angus picked up her wrist, feeling for her pulse.

"Do you want anything?"

"Go away."

"Tea or something? A piece of toast?"

Silently, Hedda turned her back on him.

Angus went into the TV room and dialled the telephone. He waited with the receiver pressed to his ear and looked out the wide windows at the grey river, swollen now with rain and rushing madly past the house.

"Dad? It's Angus. Mom's gone off again."

---

During Hedda's bouts of depression she stayed in bed, sometimes for weeks, her fingers curled, lean and tough as roots, over the edge of the sheet. There was nothing for them to do but ride it out. Analysis didn't seem to help and antidepressants were too dangerous. Hedda had overdosed on them so many times that no psychiatrist would prescribe them for her any more. As long as Hedda stayed in bed, Dempster took leave from work. He made the boys' lunches, hung the laundry out to flap in the river breeze, whistled as he swept the house, played Beethoven on the stereo, watered Hedda's geraniums, baked pound cakes, made soothing meals of stew, chili con carne, chicken potpie.

"You must hate me," Hedda told him. "I don't know why you stick around."

"Nonsense," Dempster said cheerfully. "This is like a holiday for me. A holiday from work. It's the only time I get to be creative."

He'd married Hedda because he believed she could save him from being just another bland civil servant. When he first spotted her at the opening of her first show, her face was so naked, so full of genius and pain that he crossed the room to speak to her. He was young, rising gracefully through the civil service. Life up until then had been too easy, too predictable. In Hedda's eyes he saw passion, a profound knowledge he knew he could never acquire on his own. He thought she could teach him to experience the world. As soon as he saw her, he knew that if he could not find a way, an opportunity to walk on that fine line between invention and annihilation, he might as well be dead.

In the weeks of Hedda's recovery, Dempster climbed the stairs hourly to her bedside, a tall, heavy man with a receptive face and lusty gaps between his teeth. The weight he'd put on bit by bit during his thirties and forties reflected an uncomplicated approach to life. He had a habit of drifting on the surface of things, of taking each day as it came. Dressed in a threadbare cardigan, baggy cotton trousers, his shirttails hanging out, he moved quietly, his old moccasin slippers falling softly on the carpeted steps. At mid-morning, he bore trays of toast and marmalade up to Hedda, pots of steaming tea. He placed the tray across Hedda's knees, licked marmalade from his fingers, opened a volume of Virginia Woolf and read out loud. His deep voice reading chapter after chapter of *To the Lighthouse* drifted out the door along with the smell of sickness permeating the house, for he kept a vapourizer going beside Hedda's bed because she liked the comforting smell of camphor. Cocooned up there with Hedda, Dempster enjoyed the warmth of the room, the confined space, the view of the fast river. He liked to watch Hedda gathering strength, to feel he was restoring her to health.

More and more, during Hedda's collapses, Garreth wanted to escape to the houses of friends.

"I thought she was like that because she was a woman" was the news he brought back to Angus, who, in his brother's absence, wandered around the house as though he'd lost a limb. "But other kids' mothers aren't like her. She's nuts!" Soon, Angus was saying to Dempster, "I think I'll go camping with Garreth and the guys this weekend. Is that all right?" he asked, biting his lip. "Will you and Mom be okay?"

When they were sixteen, the boys bought with their savings an old Chevy convertible, in which they tore off to matinees, football games, the pool hall. Dempster waved them off, then stood on the porch and watched the Chevy disappear around the corner, envying a little their youth, their irresponsibility, their happiness.

Then, driven by the silence of the house out onto the second-storey deck, he sat for hours in a thick Aran sweater, looking at the sky, the trees, the cobalt river flashing in the sunlight, the blackbirds swooping down with open beaks as if to scoop up diamonds from its glittering surface. The wind lifted his thin grey hair and turned the pages of an unread novel lying open across his knee. He tried simply to enjoy the scene, the purity of the steadfast river with its transparent and unchanging course, the willows, whose branches seemed to gather up all his sorrows like a flock of songless swallows. He began to understand that what he now longed for in life was simplicity, a little peace, but the events of their lives, the fits, the wrist-slashings, the stepping in front of moving buses, the destruction, began to pile up in his memory, pressing down like a great weight on his shoulders, his chest.

Hedda, waking at four o'clock in the afternoon, said to him, "I love to see you out there when I open my eyes. It's such a comfort to me. Your back is so strong, braced against the wind. You're like a fortress, protecting me from harm." And Dempster thanked God that Hedda had not noticed his body shaking with despair.

Sooner or later Hedda would emerge from the bedroom, allowing Dempster to return to work. She'd fly into a fit of industry. She might spend the next weeks cooking up vats of vegetable soup. She bought gallons of paint and coloured the rooms of the house oxblood, chartreuse, Wedgwood blue, mustard. She painted a landscape of green hills and cloudlike sheep on the front door window. She refinished furniture, marched in political rallies, wrote letters to the papers about nuclear arms, refugees, acid rain. All of this was good therapy. It made her feel sane again, so that one day she had the courage once more to open the cellar door, which had remained closed since her collapse. She descended the stairs, from which Dempster had swept up all sign of destruction, and began again.

Of course they never knew how long she would be well. The spring the boys turned eighteen, on a day of fine April showers, Dempster arrived home from work to a dark house. He had not expected to see the boys, they had jobs after school at the local video store, but there was no sign of Hedda either. He stood in the front hall and listened, the chill of the rooms going through him. He knew what the silence in the house meant, that he should, at this very instant, begin collecting all of his energies to meet whatever drama was about to unfold, but he felt only an overwhelming fatigue and a powerlessness. Turning, looking through the open door at the wet street, the dripping trees, he contemplated running out again into the afternoon, where the soft rainfall might wash over him like a healing bath, absolve him of obligation, cleanse Hedda from his life.

But then a crash came from below, something overturning in the basement, and Dempster knew that he had waited a moment too long for escape. A lifetime of habit made him drop his briefcase, throw open the cellar door, thunder down the stairs two at a time. There he saw, illuminated by the weak silver light falling from the high windows, Hedda hanging by her neck from a beam, her body turning gracefully, like a mobile stirred by a gentle wind.

"Jesus Christ, Hedda!" Dempster shouted. Then, trembling, stumbling, weeping, blinded by tears, he seized a crate and pushed it across the ancient earth floor. Heaped on a nearby table were Hedda's tools. He made a frantic search through them, flinging chisels, brushes, hammers aside until he found a long sharp knife she employed to cut off hunks of raw clay from a great block. He leapt up onto the crate and gripped Hedda around the waist, reached up and sawed the rope in half. The full weight of her body fell into his arms, almost insupportable, killing. He very nearly toppled over with her off the crate. But, steadying himself, he managed to ease her down onto the dusty floor. He gripped her thin face in his hands and pressed his mouth to hers. He blew a gust of air into her throat, turned his head and watched her chest for signs of movement, repeated the process again, and again. He may have hoped that she would not revive, that this was to be the final scene. He tasted the bitterness of her lips, smelled the musty odour of the basement coming off her hair, her clothes. But then her chest did heave, she coughed and wheezed and returned to life. Dempster knelt on the floor beside her and wept into his hands.

"Too bad she didn't kill herself," said Garreth angrily that night. "She never goes quite far enough, does she? She'd rather destroy the rest of us." He went out that evening with a large suitcase, saying he was going to live with a friend. The next morning Hedda woke to see Dempster dressing for work.

"You're not staying home?" she said.

"I wish I could, but they're making the announcement about the promotion sometime this week. I could risk losing the portfolio if I'm not visible."

"You should have let me die."

"Perhaps."

"I'm sorry."

"I'll call you from the office if I get a chance."

"Will *you* stay with me, then?" she asked Angus.

"I've got school, Mom," he said apologetically. "Easter exams. They're important. They could make or break my university entrance."

The rain had stopped, though the air was heavy with moisture. From her bed, Hedda could smell the sweet, pungent spring earth. Listening to the empty house, she heard more than silence. She smelled abandonment. It occurred to her for the first time that if she did not get up, Dempster and Angus might never come home. She rose then, with the mark from the hanging rope dark as an amethyst choker around her throat. She put on her clothes, called Joseph and told him she wanted another exhibition, went down the cellar stairs and picked up her tools. She believed that her creativity would draw her family back to her, just as long ago it had pulled Dempster across the gallery to introduce himself to her, shy and hopeful. She had to believe it. And she was right. This time she was right. That evening the two of them, Dempster and Angus, did trickle in quietly. Descending the cellar stairs, cautious, prepared for disaster, they found her firing up her kiln, clay in her hair.

"I feel so wonderful," she assured them. "I don't remember ever wanting so much to—to live."

Through the summer, Hedda toiled long days, ate more heartily than she had in years, slept only a few hours each night before returning to her studio. Some afternoons, she worked out on the back porch, painting her clay scenes. In the pearly midday, the river-bank was moist and green and the distant towers of the city like a hazy blue watercolour. Hedda breathed deeply, filling her lungs with the river air. Mixing her clay, she heard the cries of children wading barefoot along the weedy bank, knee-deep among the lily pads, looking for bullfrogs. The old white footbridge, spanning the river like a Gothic flying buttress, threw its lacy reflection across the water. Charles, asleep in the sun at Hedda's feet, snored through the afternoons. Now Angus was working evenings. Dempster, arriving home from the office to find the Chevy idle in the driveway, was free to go for a spin through the soft night, the top down, while Hedda made moulds and bases and fired her compositions in the kiln.

"Tell Garreth I'm so much better," she said often to Angus that summer. "Will you tell him for me?"

"He knows it, Mom," answered Angus patiently. "I told him already."

"Then why doesn't he come home and see me?" she asked, but he could only smile at her sheepishly, and Hedda saw that he did not believe she could be happy for long, that with Hedda nothing lasted forever. And even Dempster, walking around the basement, surveying the show she was putting together, seemed to drift at a safe distance from her. "Well, you really have been working terribly hard. Your pieces—as always, your pieces are quite amazing," he said, but his voice was light and disengaged, guarded.

The day before Hedda's exhibition, Dempster called Garreth on the phone. "Maybe your mother has turned a corner," he told Gar-reth happily. "I hardly recognize her these days. She seems to be a new woman. Will you at least come to the opening? An appearance by you could make all the difference."

Garreth showed up at the gallery looking handsome in his friend's sports coat. He drank too much red wine and would not let Hedda touch him. Hungry for the sight of his profile, she watched him through the crowd. Moving around the gallery, looking at her pieces, Garreth said to Angus, "Remember those days in the kitchen after school? Remember how these things used to bring us such happiness? Now they just make me feel dead inside."

Joseph produced a camera, motioned for the four of them to stand together so that he could take a picture. "I'm not standing in any fuckin' picture with *her*!" Garreth said, and he pushed his way across the room and through the door.

Out on the sidewalk, he noticed the wineglass still in his hand and threw it against the gallery wall. Hedda tried to follow him but a cluster of reviewers closed in on her. Dempster went out and picked the pieces of glass up off the sidewalk.

"Every last piece sold," Joseph told Hedda excitedly at the end of the evening, but she did not seem to be listening.

The next day she carried everything up out of her studio and into the backyard.

"What's Mom doing?" Angus asked Garreth, who had come home to pack all his belongings for university. They were to leave together in three days. They stood at an upper window and watched her throw a live match onto the heap of paint cans, plywood, moulds, tools. The pile burst into flame, a paint can exploded. Angus made for the door, but Garreth tackled him from behind, wrestled him to the ground and pinned him there.

"Leave her alone!" he growled into Angus's ear. "If we're lucky, the stupid bitch will set *herself* on fire!"

When the fire trucks arrived Hedda ran indoors. Angus met the fire chief on the front porch.

"Is that your mother in there?" he asked Angus. "She's pretty upset. We got a call from the neighbours about the fire. Why would she want to do a thing like this?" He searched Angus's face with concern. "Maybe you should go in and see how she is. Will you be all right with her? Are there any neighbours who could help? What about your father? We'll get rid of the crowd for you."

Angus called Dempster and told him about the fire. "No, she's not hurt. But we need you here. She likes to know you're in the house. So will you get here as soon as you can?"

But, Dempster didn't come home at all that night.

"Where's you father?" asked Hedda the next morning when Angus brought her an omelette in bed.

"Maybe he had to go out of town or something," said Angus, his expression confused, frightened.

Angus called Dempster's office again and left a message but Dempster stayed away another night.

Hedda managed to get herself out of bed by the time Dempster's reflection fell on the river as he crossed the footbridge at noon the next day. The image of his white shirt floated across the water like a cloud. At the end of the bridge he turned right and headed, not down the street, but along the river path. Crossing the narrow strip of park he entered the house through the glass room, the door that was never locked. Hedda, who was on her knees in the kitchen mixing clay in a plastic tub, turned, startled.

"I thought you were a burglar."

"I forgot my key."

"I didn't hear the cab."

"There was no cab. I walked. I had a lot to think about."

He stood there with the sun on his back and the river shining behind him like a luminous ribbon. The water, in the curves of the river, was now yellow and scummy with algae. In the thick jungle of bullrushes, insects buzzed, stupid with the heat.

Dempster stepped over Charles, asleep on the floor and blocking the kitchen door. He shoved his hands unhappily into his pockets. Hedda held her breath and waited, kneeling with both hands bearing down on the plastic tub for support.

"I'm going to have to leave you, Hedda," Dempster said.

"Oh."

Hedda stood up then and wiped the clay powder from her

hands. She was wearing a white shirt with the collar open, revealing her frail neck. Perhaps she had expected Dempster and had put on this fresh blouse to meet him. He tried not to look at her lovely throat, at her slender thighs, which were unexpectedly sensuous in tight jeans.

"Maybe you're feeling restless because the boys are leaving," she suggested. "That should pass. It's a change, something we can get used to."

"That's not it. It has nothing to do with the boys."

"What, then?"

"I don't know what you want in life, Hedda. I don't know any more what to do for you. That fire you set after the show. You've never been more successful. But you had to destroy that. You have to push everything to the edge. I'm not sure I've been good for you. I think you have to decide for yourself whether you're going to live or die."

They both looked sad and apologetic and a little incredulous, because, after all they'd been through, she could not believe—and he too, he could not quite believe—that he was leaving her. After all those times he'd pulled her back from the brink, he was leaving her now, when she was up on her feet, dressed in a crisp blouse, apparently whole and lucid, her hands covered with productive clay?

"I just feel—I'm just so tired, Hedda."

She said, "I'm willing to try harder. I'll go back into therapy—"

"No, Hedda."

"Maybe there's another pill—"

"Hedda, stop!" He turned then and crossed the room, a little impatient, frowning. He looked restlessly out at the river. Hedda, noticing for the first time the fine lines on his face, illuminated by the bright reflection from the water, was shocked to see the toll exacted by the events of their life together. He was nearly fifty. She knew he had to get out now.

"There's another complication," he said unhappily.

39

"A woman?"

"Yes."

"Ah."

Hedda smiled sadly to herself. "When did it happen?" she asked, as though knowing the exact sequence of events might help her understand.

"I don't know," said Dempster, looking guilty, confused. "Months ago. It was one day when I was out in the Chevy. It was spring."

———————

The day after Dempster left, Hedda closed the door to the cellar, pressed her forehead against the rough wood and prayed, though she did not know to whom. She waited for the fall to come. She wanted something to change, to mark off from the past this new stage in her life, but summer wouldn't leave. She longed for rain and wind and cold weather and coloured leaves but they didn't come. It occurred to her that this might be some kind of test, some trick, calculated to confuse. Life seemed full of tricks now. She had to be careful.

In the air there was a sense of dangerous ripeness and a feeling of both luck and impatience at this gift of a prolonged summer. The gardens were saturated with colour, the flowers threatened to explode, and the apples, heavy in the backyard tree, still refused to drop. Through September, the reflection of the willows in the glass room was so convincing that birds flew against the windows all day long, killing themselves. Daily, Hedda found their stiff little bodies on the porch and buried them in the garden. She saw people passing along the river, pedestrians and cyclists on the dirt path hugging the bank, so many people passing. For the first time in her life, she wondered who all these people were and where they were going.

Walking with Charles along the river one Saturday, Hedda ran into Dempster, accompanied by a woman. He didn't know what to say.

"Look at this fall we're having, Hedda!" he cried, embarrassed, ridiculously cheerful. It was October and finally the leaves were in full colour. "I never knew autumn was such a beautiful season!" He introduced his companion as Suzie and Hedda wondered if a grown woman could really be called that. Suzie was somewhere in her thirties, healthy, energetic, with straight brown bangs and a perky ponytail. Hedda marvelled at her wholeness, her contentment, her smooth face. She looked entirely unscathed by life. She smiled kindly at Hedda and walked on a little further, leaving Dempster and Hedda to talk.

"She's very pretty," said Hedda. Dempster reddened, objected mildly.

"It's not her prettiness, it's—she's so—she's just so damned happy. Hedda, I—"

"Do you hear from the boys?"

"Yes. They send their love, of course. They do love you. Never doubt that." As he spoke, Dempster was patting Charles soundly on the head, scratching him under the chin, rubbing his big floppy ears, all the while unable to take his eyes off Hedda.

She said, "I thought at least Angus—"

"Angus—even Angus has a lot of healing to do."

Walking home with Charles, Hedda said, "Well, what do you think of her, Charles? She seems to be making Dempster very happy. Are you sure you don't want to go and live with them? Join the great exodus? She looks like she might be a dog lover."

In November, Hedda put on a coat and went out onto the second-storey deck to pull the geraniums up out of her big clay pots. She tied string around their roots so that she could take them in the house and hang them upside down over the winter. While she was working with the string, she heard Charles bark. Looking down, she saw him racing across the narrow park to greet Dempster, who was passing by.

"How are you doing, old soldier?" Dempster's voice drifted across the yellowed grass and up to Hedda. He clapped Charles on the back. "You old trooper! Where do you get your energy?" Hedda continued tying her string. Then, feeling Dempster's eyes on her, sensing his curiosity, his guilt, she withdrew to the house and watched him walk away down the dusty path, throwing glances over his shoulder at the house.

The first snow fell early in December. Hedda, removing the curtains on the deck windows to wash them, pushed aside the sliding door, bent and scooped up a handful of light, fresh snow. She pressed it to her cheek, felt its purity, its numbing cold. She placed her hand flat on the cool glass and looked out at a film of ice forming on the river. When he was packing his bags in September, Dempster had said to her, "I always wondered why you never tried to drown yourself in the river. It's so obvious and so handy. I would think it would be a gentle way to go, after all the things you've tried."

In January Hedda worked in the kitchen, potting up narcissus, daffodils, crocuses, in anticipation of spring. She rubbed the moist black earth between her fingers, raised it to her nostrils, sniffed and thought about her clay. She refinished the kitchen table, running her hand over and over the aged wood, warm as flesh in the winter sun. She mended curtains that had needed attention for decades, scraped the old wax off the wide floorboards. It came up in great yellow curls. She worked not with her old manic pace, but slowly, reflectively, while Charles followed her from room to room. If she could just keep herself grounded this way, in touch with all the surfaces, the textures of the house, she thought an existence might just be possible for her.

Then one day in February, when she was upstairs watching workmen cutting keys on the river to prevent spring flooding, the telephone rang.

"Mom?" a voice at once foreign and achingly familiar came over the wire. "Mom, it's Angus. Do you know where Dad is? I've been trying to reach him."

"No. What's wrong?"

"His office said he was on a holiday. It's urgent. Garreth has slashed his wrists."

"Where is he?" asked Hedda. "I'll come at once."

"You can't, Mom," said Angus gently. "He doesn't want to see you. He made that very clear. It's not that he doesn't love you, Mom. It's just that he's afraid of the effect you have on him. He's afraid he's like you. I guess he's known that for a long time. It's Dad he needs right now."

Joseph came to visit her that afternoon. He found her upstairs looking out the window, where the men, working with winches, were drawing great plugs of blue ice out of the river and lining them up, forming what looked like a primitive and mysterious monument.

"I look out at this scene," she said to Joseph. "The river, the park, the trees. I don't understand how everything can be so beautiful, and yet I can't be happy within it. I look out and I see people leading such simple, steady lives and I wonder how they can do it. There was so much potential for all of us to be happy here on the river, in this comfortable old house, but I made it impossible. What am I going to do? My family is gone. I've nearly destroyed my son."

"You're going to get out your clay and start making art again," said Joseph gently. He was small, quiet, elegantly dressed, a white-haired man of sixty years. He looked very lonely. It was the first time Hedda had ever noticed this. Possibly he'd always looked lonely. He was a bachelor. She wondered if anyone had ever loved him.

"I feel sick when I think Garreth is going to live the same cycle I've been through."

"If he does," said Joseph, "so be it. Hedda, you've got to stop wishing your life had been different. You have to accept that this is the journey you were meant to take. The attempted suicides, Dempster leaving, the estrangement of your children, all of this was in the cards for you from the day you were born and all of it has its own necessary place in your life. If you could just embrace that, maybe you would find a measure of happiness."

———————

Then it was fall again and the suns in the evenings were pink and the river had a pink skin. Hedda was out when Dempster came to see her, but he sat patiently on the sagging couch in the sunroom, with one hand resting on Charles's old head, until she came in around dinnertime, carrying two paper bags of groceries, which she set on the kitchen counter. The movement of his rising from the couch caught her eye. She wasn't as surprised to see him as he thought she'd be.

"Hello," she said neutrally, as if she'd found another dead bird on the porch blinded by an illusion of free passage through willow trees. She was wearing a longish tan skirt buttoned as far down as her knee, a pale blue blouse, a creamy vest. She looked younger, healthy and strong. The stark white parting down the middle of her hair reminded Dempster of a seagull's feather.

She remembered Dempster standing there, both of them standing there exactly like this a little more than a year ago—the open door through which he'd silently stepped, his figure filling the kitchen doorway before she even heard him, the water shining behind him, a river of light.

It was a breezy afternoon. Outside, a golden rain was now falling from the willow trees. The sweet, heavy smell of apples, rotting in the long, cold grass, drifted in through the windows. Hedda had thought, every day for a year she had thought about what she'd say if Dempster ever came back. She'd thought she had something prepared, but now she only said, "You've gained weight."

Dempster laughed ruefully, looking down at himself. "I know. I look terrible."

"No, you don't," she said quickly. "Really. Your face—your face looks younger this way. No, you look good." She sounded so fragile and innocent, she looked so *wronged* that Dempster hated himself for leaving her. He glanced around, impressed.

"You've been working hard."

"For a few months."

She could have told him that she had a dealer in Toronto now, and that another one in Vancouver was taking a serious look at her work. This was what she'd thought she might tell him if he'd come to the gallery, to her recent show. But she didn't say it now. It was still good news, but it belonged to her.

Dempster stepped forward, anxious to speak. "I wondered," he said. "I wondered about moving back in with you."

"You've got tired of this Suzie, then?"

Dempster laughed, laughed at himself. "I'm not sure she needs me. She has such equilibrium. I have the feeling all the time that if I weren't there, she'd be just as happy. Maybe we're too much like each other. Life can get dull in that sort of relationship. Suzie doesn't have your depths, Hedda. I miss the intensity of living with you."

Hedda looked around at the kitchen. For some time she'd been working there. Why stay in the basement when she had the whole house to herself? There was clay everywhere, cans of paint, vats of water, tools, the plywood she cut up to make bases, a saw leaning in a corner, drifts of sawdust on the floor, lumber in the hallway for the construction of shipping crates.

Dempster read her mind. "I love things just the way they are," he assured her. "I always missed you when you worked downstairs. I always felt cut off. This way I could watch you. I don't care about the mess. No, really, it's perfect this way."

Hedda looked at him, dangerously tempted. Of course she still

45

loved him. There was nothing she wanted more than to take him back. But she said, "You were right. The only way I can survive is to depend on myself. If you come back, I'll start to rely on you. I'm afraid of your strength. I know now that I can't live with anyone. I'm ready to accept that. I've got a new prescription. I'm stable enough to keep myself from eating a bottle of pills in one sitting."

"But you're alone here. You can't be happy."

"Perhaps not. But I feel more at peace with myself than ever before. I'm not lonely. My mind keeps my heart company. This seems to be as good as life gets."

Soon, she thought, she'd have enough money to buy out Dempster's interest in the house. This was the best place for her, here where the light was palpable, the air musical with the cricket's song, and the river flowed by, with its power to give life and to take it away.

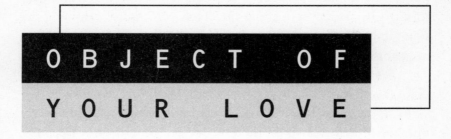

# OBJECT OF YOUR LOVE

"**A**ND, DEAR LORD," says my brother Floyd at dinner, "let us pray for our beloved father, who is in exile in the United States, and hope that he'll return to us some day."

"You don't know *where* he is," I say. "For all you know he's dead."

Mother, Floyd and his wife Blanche raise their eyes warily and look at me. It is a September evening and their faces are thrown back into the room by the black kitchen windows: Floyd with his brittle Christian smile disclosing a mouthful of tiny rotting teeth, Blanche batting her fleshy eyelids at me in disapproval, Mother swallowing a small, anxious, let's-not-fight gulp of air. Blanche and Floyd grip Mother's bony hands in prayer, holding her arms high, like a prize-fighter in a boxing ring. Mother wears the expression of surprise and reluctant salvation of a suicide victim pulled from a river. She joined Floyd's church a year ago.

"You brought us up as atheists," I reminded her at the time. "How can you go against everything you ever taught us?"

She shrugged. "It's made my life easier. Floyd doesn't pester me any more. Maybe you should consider it yourself."

"I'd sooner take poison."

Ten years ago Father ran away. At the time, I was twenty, Floyd twenty-five. Weeks after he disappeared we realized he'd taken

Floyd's credit card with him. We were able to trace his progress through the States by reading the credit card bill: a gasoline purchase in Watertown, New York. Dinner in Syracuse. Motel rooms in Pennsylvania, Maryland, Virginia.

"He's following the Interstate 81," I said, examining an atlas. "He's taking his time. Probably headed for Florida."

"I hope he's not ill," Mother fretted, referring to a pharmacy purchase that appeared on the bill. She is a simple, unquestioning woman who does not always grasp the magnitude of things.

"Now," said Blanche with extraordinary insight, "we'll be able to tell people we have relatives in Florida."

Floyd said he wasn't angry with Father for running up his credit card bill. "He didn't mean any harm," he said.

"Floyd," I shook my head, "you are a simpleton."

"If you were in touch with God," he smiled at me with gentle pity, "you'd know how to forgive." Floyd is small, fastidious, womanish, tiny-boned, a physical weakling with round wire-rimmed glasses and a red goatee. He has grown a beard because he thinks it makes him look biblical, but he lacks the moral presence of a holy man.

Floyd got religion in his early twenties. He was working then at the dairy. He became so crazed with God that he marched around the dairy crying, "Praise the Lord, brother! Hallelujah, sister!" his face blazing with religious fervour. He sang hymns on the job. He tried to get a prayer group going at lunch break. One day he put proselytizing flyers in the empty milk bottles riding down the conveyor belt. That was when they fired him.

Now he is a lay preacher in the Church of the Risen Christ. He assists the minister: opens the church up on Sundays, greets worshippers at the door, counts the collection money, that sort of thing. He teaches Sunday school and gives the Scripture readings at services. Once in a while, they let him give a sermon. For this, they pay him a small salary.

Floyd and Blanche have a tiny apartment over near the bus depot but they are always at our place. The apartment, they say, makes them restless, there's nothing to do there. I can't blame them for being bored with each other. Floyd reads the Bible all day and Blanche wants to watch television but their set is broken. At our house, she turns on the TV and sinks down onto the sofa, an enormous woman with long black hairs clinging like spiders to the corners of her mouth. Her body is, itself, like a piece of furniture in its cumbersomeness and inertia, its soft preponderance. She is like an armchair swollen with cotton wadding. All afternoon she watches the game shows, a plate of Mother's lemon squares balanced on her knee.

"They need a child to distract them," Mother says of Blanche and Floyd.

"They're children themselves," I tell her.

"And, brethren," Floyd says at dinner, his eyelids fluttering with piety, "let us bow our heads once more, for we are not finished with the Lord's work at this table. We will pray for our sister, Jean, that she may open her heart to the love of God—"

I push my chair back. "I'll take my plate to my room rather than sit here listening to this rot."

"Before you go," interrupts Blanche, "could you pass the mashed potatoes?"

Around nine o'clock, I hear the front door close. I go to the head of the stairs. "Are the idiots gone?" I call down.

"Do you mean Blanche and Floyd?" replies Mother.

Once, I thought they'd left and they hadn't. "Are the idiots gone?" I called down.

"No," Blanche answered without thinking. "We're still here."

----

On the weekends, Mother and I lead a quiet life. Mother rises late and drifts from room to room in her mules and thick flannelette

49

nightgown. She stands at the kitchen window, motionless, looking out at Father's bird feeder, at the chickadees, cardinals, blue jays, the hardy, faithful birds who will abide the Canadian winter with us. Their bright wings, their swiftness, their greed entertain her. For a long time she stands fixed at the window, thinking no doubt of Father, perhaps believing that as long as we feed the birds in his stead, there is hope that one day he will fly back to us.

Pressed to the cold windowsill as though frozen there, Mother's fingers turn as white as bones. A circle of vapour forms on the glass where her face comes close to it, her lips moving in silent entreaty. Later, she sits in her swivel rocker and says her prayers, reading from a small scarlet book. Around noon she takes a bath in an inch of tepid water. "Fill the tub up," I call to her through the bathroom door. "Pour in the hot. Spoil yourself. Enjoy your bath." "I don't want to waste water," she says. Her skin has gotten very thin, slippery and loose. Like an old silk suit that doesn't fit her any more, it ripples and sags. On the backs of her hands, there are big brown spots the size of coppers. She can pinch the skin there and pull it away a distance of an inch. The hair has fallen out of her arms and legs. She is smooth as a newborn baby.

After lunch, she puts on her clothes, thin sweaters that do not keep her warm. Thick ones are too heavy, she says, she cannot support their punishing weight. They exhaust her. In her inadequate cardigan, she shivers, rises to turn up the thermostat on the living-room wall. She sits again in her chair and reads large-print books borrowed from the library, blinking at the heavy black lettering, her legs extended straight out in front of her, her heels, supported by a footstool, pressed together, the toes of her shoes pointing up at the ceiling. She reaches to turn on the radio.

In our kitchen cupboards there are tins of peanut brittle, cookies with a dot of strawberry jam in the centre, bags of jelly beans, Oh Henry chocolate bars. These are the things Mother wants. She eats very little. Though she can't finish dinner, at the end of the meal she

50

always says, "What is there for dessert? I have to have something sweet with my tea." Her day builds up into this little hill with something sweet on the top. Outside of sugar, she is not interested in food. She says she can't taste anything, is never hungry. It is as though her system is dormant, as though all her bodily functions have ground to a halt. No longer does she perspire or menstruate or get up in the night to relieve herself.

———————

Late on a wet, dark September afternoon, I am reviewing inventory before a large window in the back room of the dentist's office where I work as an assistant. The office is downtown, just off King Street, in an old, picturesque Victorian house with peaked gables and white spindle porch rails. It is a cozy office, with crooked walls, modern, muted lighting, small, impractical examination rooms, soft music floating from invisible speakers, grey silencing broadloom on the floors.

It is 5:15. Dr. Peter Beveridge steps into the room and closes in behind me, swift and silent as a leopard after its prey. "Everyone's gone home," he whispers into the hollow of my neck. I myself have heard the last of the staff preparing to leave, the singing of empty coat hangers set swinging on the cloakroom rod, the hum of the evening traffic flowing in through the front door as it is opened again and again. *Good night, good night.*

Dr. Peter Beveridge spreads his hands on my hips with much the same professional authority I have seen him employ in pressing rebellious patients into the dental chair. On my neck I feel his breath, which smells, I have noticed recently, like the powders he packs into the dental cavities of his patients. The scent is on his fingers, it seems to come out of his pores. I have a mental picture of this compound slowly flowing through his veins, a white, chalky substance.

"I want you to leave Mrs. Beveridge," I say without turning

around. We are reflected together in the windowpane before us, he a foot taller than I and brilliant as light in his white smock. Recently he has holidayed in Mexico, returning with his face bronzed and healthy. I look at his reflection and shake with desire. For three years I have worshipped him like a god: his height, his powerful shoulders, his square, clean jaw, his moist, brown eyes, his sculptured hair, his tan, his good fortune, his income.

Dr. Peter Beveridge sighs. "Oh, Jean," he says gently but firmly. He is fifteen years older than I and sometimes talks to me as though he were my father or my analyst. "You feel depressed today," he tells me. "It's just the rain." We are looking out the window at the bank parking lot next door, where a diagonal rain is falling and the wind has driven huge orange leaves flat against a wire fence.

"It's not the rain," I say impatiently. In the parking lot, cars arrive and depart, their headlights shining in the gathering dusk. People run in and out of the bank, their collars turned up against the weather. Through the enormous plate-glass bank windows, I can see the customers shuffling forward between crimson ropes to the tall counters, talking to the tellers, carrying on their common, innocent transactions, preparing to dash out once more to their cars and drive home in the steady, inching traffic, cook dinner, turn on their television sets, spend the evening with their husbands and wives and children. That is all I want, I think: a normal life.

If I let him, Dr. Beveridge will draw me out to reception, where there are warm lights and a long couch, behind which, in a large aquarium, jewel-coloured fish glide slowly through illuminated water. The fish have a tranquillizing effect on patients, especially those coming to us for invasive procedures such as extractions, implants, crowns. Dr. Peter Beveridge will snap the front door lock, pull the drapes in the bow window overlooking the street, hang the Closed sign on the door, like a shopkeeper preparing to take inventory. He will lay me down on the couch and apply himself to me while the fish swim round and round.

Soon I will find that I am not thinking about the skilful progress of his hands or what is happening on another more disturbing level, the level of feeling. I am not connected to him or to myself at all. Rather, I am concentrating on the fish, memorizing their shapes and colours, the incandescent black, orange, yellow, purple, blue dots and stripes. It is less alarming, less complicated to follow their calm circuit than to focus on Dr. Peter Beveridge's body, now beginning to heave and quake on top of me, to offer its shameless, grateful, plaintive whimpers. The fish regard me with candid, immobile eyes, sway and turn, press their wide flat lips against the glass, blow mocking bubbles at me. And I, in turn, pity them in their watery prison, am numbed by their slow, perpetual motion.

Dr. Beveridge tells me that he is sick. He is sick of dentistry. He wants to spend the balance of his life duck hunting. He is fed up with tooth rot and halitosis and cash flow and mortgages. He is weary of his beautiful wife, Alice, who is, he says, so good, so perfect that she makes life seem intolerable.

Sometimes Mrs. Beveridge drops into the office to speak to Dr. Beveridge. I see her walking down the carpeted hallway in her simple, quiet, expensive clothes: wool hound's-tooth slacks, a cashmere blazer, thick, cable sweater, a pair of highly polished loafers. I cannot stop staring at her, at her flawless, olive skin, her dimples deep enough to hold a penny, her large dark eyes, her cap of straight, shiny hair. She is like a beautiful doe, I think. I believe that if I were to replace her, if I were to be the new Mrs. Dr. Peter Beveridge, I would become like her: deep, gentle, wise, translucent, calm.

———————

One evening in September, Dr. Beveridge telephones me at home. He never calls me there, and I can tell that Mrs. Beveridge must be standing at his elbow because he speaks in a formal way. Would I

53

consider babysitting for them that evening? It is asking a lot, he acknowledges, it is very short notice, he is afraid I might have some social event of my own to occupy me (here, he is being—something—cute? ironic? unkind?). Their scheduled babysitter has cancelled on them and there is a function they must attend. I would be doing them an immense favour.

I eat an early dinner with Mother and then walk across town in the dark, through deep, dusty drifts of leaves to their house. I am excited about seeing Dr. Beveridge on a weekend night, about getting a look at the inside of his house for the first time, about being near him in his wife's presence because this seems to me cheeky and iniquitous. I feel jittery and treacherous and aroused and ashamed. I am too dressed up for babysitting, having put on a silk blouse, short skirt, black nylons, black suede high heels. One of his sons (age ten) answers the door and then Mrs. Beveridge comes forward with her white smile and her kind, trusting face.

"Oh, Jean," she says, taking my hand warmly. "This is so good of you." She is discreetly attired in low pumps, a simple black wool crêpe dress, small drop earrings. Her beauty is pure and true and natural and sustaining, like clear springwater. I may at this moment love her as much as I think I love Dr. Beveridge.

The house, a long, low bungalow, is just as I imagined it would be—elegant but unpretentious: low, pearly light, champagne broadloom, white leather couches, long expanses of sheer-draped window. Serenity. Silence like a cocoon, all sound absorbed by the finger-deep carpet and the raw-silk wallpaper.

Into the living room Mrs. Beveridge leads me, where there are many people standing about in intimate clusters, drinking cocktails and eating fancy morsels of food before they all go out together to this important dinner.

"Everybody!" she says, calling their attention to me. "This is Jean, Peter's assistant. She's saved our lives tonight. She's staying with the boys."

They all turn then, garmented in silk and dark suits and ruffled shirts and bow ties. With a critical arching of their eyebrows, they appraise my inappropriate clothes, they smile coldly at me as if to say, Well, if she's the babysitter, what's she doing in here with *us*? I feel foolish, unworthy, raked over by their eyes. Then Dr. Beveridge says to me in a businesslike tone, "Come, Jean, I'll show you the boys' rooms. This way."

I follow him down a long, carpeted hallway. However, we never reach the boys' rooms because Dr. Beveridge turns and pushes me into the master bedroom, swiftly, silently pulling the door closed behind us. He calls me a beautiful bitch, though I am not beautiful at all, I am homely. Maybe the bitch part is true, though. Like a wild animal, he tears at my blouse. I watch a button fly across the room, hear a seam give way. With his great professional teeth, he bites my neck, my shoulders, my breasts. Pain shoots through my body. I should, I tell myself, be pleased by this turn of events, for though I had not dared to hope for this opportunity, this little bonus, little tip for the serviceable babysitter, hadn't I prayed for something in this vein?

But now I find myself looking around, full of envy and curiosity, cataloguing the contents of the bedroom, observing Mrs. Beveridge's silver hairbrush on the dresser, her designer jeans draped across a small, sweet upholstered chair that looks like it was meant for a doll's house, the closet doors standing open and her dresses hanging there, pressed intimately against Dr. Beveridge's suits, the thick pocket novel lying open on the low, wide waterbed. Presently, Dr. Beveridge, satiated, recovers himself, smooths his coiffure, straightens his bow tie in the mirror, pats me territorially on the behind and slips gracefully out into the hall, returning to his friends, leaving the door slightly ajar. Their ugly, explosive laughter tumbles in on me as I crawl on my hands and knees across the carpet, searching for my button and flapping my blouse to dry his slobber off it so that I can go out and find the boys' rooms for myself.

When I am putting him to bed, Eric, the son who answered the door, says, "Do you work for my father?" He is a serious, fair boy with a round, intelligent, gourdlike head.

"Yes," I answer. "I'm his dental assistant."

"What do you do?"

"I keep the examination room organized," I explain readily. "I hand him whatever instruments he needs to work with. I mix the preparations he uses in the patients' mouths."

"That sounds boring," Eric tells me.

"It's not boring," I say, somewhat defensive. "It's interesting. You have to be very organized. You have to be quite intelligent to be a dental assistant."

He scrutinizes me calmly. "You don't *look* intelligent."

---

Dr. Beveridge says to me, "Jean, you're driving me crazy!" because I have told him, "Keep your hands off of me. If you touch me, I'll scream at the top of my lungs. I mean it."

"Jean, don't do this to me."

"Leave her and you can have me again," I say.

"I am the hunter and you are a little purple-winged duck," he used to tell me, and he'd pursue me all day long. Little pinches and strokes as I squeezed past him in the examination room. Nicks and bites between patients. Mouth against my neck. Finger down my collar. Finger driven hard into my armpit like the cold rigid barrel of a gun. Knuckle riding down my spine. Hot breath in my hair. Lips brushing my ear. Fingers up the sleeve of my uniform at the X-ray station. A hand down my front in the supply room. In the empty staff room, a hand shooting, swift as an arrow, up under my skirt and inside my panties. Fingernails raking at my pubic hair.

And I was supposed to keep working. That was my instruction. I was not to flinch or jump or shiver or blush or indicate in any way my arousal. I was to go on mixing up the platinum in a little dish, sliding the tiny pieces of X-ray film into their sleeves, placing gleaming probes in notches around the circular instrument table, fastening paper bibs around the patients' necks, as though nothing had happened. That was part of the game. There was this buildup, this mounting of desire until the office emptied out and he had his way with me on the sofa, the love couch, where all day long the patients had sat innocently reading *Ladies Home Journal* or watching the circling fish, later silent witnesses to our passion.

"I want to be something more important to you than a game," I tell Dr. Beveridge. "I'm tired of being your toy."

"Oh, Jean. Jean, you're not a toy," he says sadly, shaking his head, his eyes so misty that I believe he is about to cry.

He tries to carry on. Leaning over his patients, his beautiful square fingers probing their mouths, he pauses and looks hungrily across their foreheads, searching my face. I sit on a high stool, with my heels hooked over the rung. I slap an instrument firmly into his extended hand and in the instant before I can release it we connect: there is an electric charge, a current running between us, through the sentient probe, with its salient, delicately curved tip. I feel the emotion of his grip, the adultery, the desire of it, the power of his maleness that set my heart pounding the first time I stood at his side. I try not to look at his immaculate hands, his manicured nails, or to watch the action of his fingers, which are long and pale and nimble as a pianist's. I catch him staring at my exposed knees. A fine perspiration forms on his upper lip. His hands begin to shake.

"Jean, you're going to ruin me," he says after the patient has left the room.

"I hope so."

One night after work, he catches my arm in the hallway, hisses in my ear, "You're acting like I don't exist, Jean!"

"You don't," I say ruthlessly, pulling on my coat. Recently I have been careful to leave the office at the same time as everyone else so

57

that he cannot apprehend me, press me, unwilling, onto the waiting-room couch. Out into the night I run with the others, into the damp fall evening with its bitter smell of dying leaves. Clattering down the wooden porch steps, I turn onto the sidewalk, away from the congestion and traffic lights of downtown, and hear my own voice, shrill, sad and gay, calling, too loud, to my co-workers, *"See you tomorrow!"*

———

On the evening of the last day in November, Dr. Beveridge says to me, "All right, Jean, you've won," and hands me a key. "I've rented a small apartment for us. It's available as of today. We'll live there on a month-to-month until things settle down and we can find something more comfortable. I'm going home now to tell Alice. You tell your family too. I'll meet you at the apartment at eight o'clock tonight. Here is the address."

Then he sweeps me off my feet, carries me out to reception and makes love to me for the first time in weeks, in the blue quivering reflections cast by the aquarium. I am in rapture. I look up at the shining fish moving in their transparent, deadly regions. Suddenly I enter, I am transported into the aquarium's landscape of sunken ships and treasure chests and tiny plastic scuba divers. My body floats, is sucked into one of the black, watery caves. I close my eyes and the searing colours of the fish burn my eyelids. I feel the fish moving over me, wave after wave of them, their scaly, wafer-thin bodies brushing the length of my limbs like feathers.

———

It is late when I arrive home.

"Jean," Mother says, relieved to see me. "It's nearly seven. We wondered." In the kitchen she and Floyd and Blanche have almost finished dinner, which is never delayed on my account because of Blanche's galloping appetite. I see that Mother has set aside something for me on a plate, covered with a pot lid.

"Too bad you came home," Blanche says, disappointed. "I was thinking of eating your dinner."

"Help yourself," I tell her indifferently. "I won't be sitting down."

"Is anything wrong, Jean?" asks Mother, worried, detecting something in my face. Floyd, his cutlery poised in the air like daggers, stops to observe me.

"She looks smug about something," says Blanche cautiously.

"Jean, sit down," says Mother, perplexed.

"I don't have time to sit down," I say. "I'm going upstairs to pack my bags. You may as well know," I tell them, "that Dr. Peter Beveridge and I have for some time been carrying on an affair. He's leaving his wife tonight. He's breaking the news to her even as we speak. We're meeting later this evening. We have an apartment waiting for us. We're going to be very happy."

There is a moment of exquisite silence while they absorb the news. Blanche's eyes are big and round, her face flattened with shock as though someone has hit her head-on with a frying pan. Mother cups her hand over her mouth.

Blanche is the first to find her voice. "I knew it!" she cries, though her soft, puddinglike face is now quivering with surprise. "I knew there was something funny going on."

"I'm glad you think it's funny," I say.

"She doesn't mean *amusing*," Floyd explains. "Jean, I'm disappointed in you."

Blanche says, "Floyd, stop her! She can't do this! How will this look at our church? She'll bring disgrace on us all."

Floyd's face has gone blank with fear. Faced with this opportunity to preach, he is nearly tongue-tied. "Jean," he says feebly, "this is a terrible thing."

"It's not terrible," I say exuberantly. "It's the most wonderful thing that has ever happened to me."

"She's gone mad," Blanche says.

"Where will you go?" asks Mother. What she means is: *will you be warm? will you eat enough? will you have a comfortable bed?* When a woman gets old, all she can remember is the advice her mother gave her, passed on by her mother before that. These are the absolutes. Dress for the weather. Don't stay up late. Wear shoes that fit. Eat green vegetables. Nothing else can be known for sure. Perhaps nothing else is worth knowing.

"You can't just walk out on Mother like this," says Blanche. "It's not right."

"Father walked out," I remind her, "and nobody seems to blame *him* for it."

"That's different," Blanche answers. "He's a man. Men get restless. There are things they have to work out of their systems."

"Oh, rot!" I say. "I've spent all my adult life doing the right thing, living here with Mother, supporting her when it was Father's job." At my words, Mother blinks rapidly and presses her lips together. "Now I'm going to do something for myself."

Reckless with joy, I go upstairs, still wearing my coat. Floyd comes after me, followed soon by Blanche, who lurks on the landing, thinking I haven't heard her heaving herself moistly up the steps. I sense her bulk on the other side of the door, like that of a large witless animal, her breath whistling through her throat, her small black eyes peering through the crack in the door.

"Jean, stop," Floyd says, his voice stern, though he is trembling with nerves. I realize for the first time that he is frightened of me but is obliged to press on because of his ministry. "Stop and think," he says. "Look before you leap. You're walking into the devil's trap."

"Spare me your sermons, Floyd," I say, pulling a suitcase from my closet. I toss it on the bed and snap it open.

"Don't cheapen yourself by doing this, Jean."

"Cheapen!" I say angrily. "What worth have I ever had to any-one around here?"

"Mother loves you" was the best he could do. Ignoring him, I tear my clothes out of the closet. Hangers fly across the room. I pull things out of drawers and fling them violently into the suitcase.

"You won't find happiness with this man," Floyd says. "It won't last. These things never do. He'll leave you eventually and all you'll be left with is your sin and your shame."

"He won't leave me," I tell him defiantly, "but I welcome the sin and the shame anyway, as they seem to be what makes life worth living."

On the other side of the door, Blanche gulps air.

---

I let myself into the apartment with the key Dr. Beveridge gave me, put my suitcases down and walk from room to room, grateful and amazed at this plain space, which is now to become my home. Turning on lights, I observe the furniture, which is sparse and threadbare. This does not bother me. On the contrary, it makes me feel purified, worthy of the simple, love-driven life on which I am embarking. I sit down at the living-room window, which overlooks the road, and for some time I stare out at the dark foreign street with its intermittent evening traffic. After a while, I get up and raise the heat on the thermostat. On another tour of the rooms, I test the taps in the bathroom, browse through the kitchen cupboards, turn on the television. Sitting down again, I wait some more. When I consult my watch, I see that it is ten o'clock. I have been here for two hours. Finally the phone rings and I grab for it.

"Jean," Dr. Beveridge's voice comes over the line. "It's me."

"I know that," I say sharply. "Where are you?"

"Jean, I'm not coming over. I can't do it," he says.

"What do you mean?"

"I can't come over there."

"Why not?"

"I swear to God, I came home with every intention of carrying through. But, Jean, I came in and the house smelled wonderful. Alice and the kids had held dinner up for me. A pot roast. Scalloped potatoes."

"I know how to make pot roast," I tell him.

"The boys were full of news about their hockey club, plans for the weekend. Everyone was so beautiful and excited. Everyone was so happy. I couldn't spoil it."

"Tell them tomorrow night, then," I say, noticing that I've begun to shake. "I've waited three years for this. Another twenty-four hours won't kill me."

"You don't understand, Jean," he says, his voice growing firmer. "Basically, we *are* a happy family. I'm not coming over there. I'm calling it off."

"Maybe you don't understand, either. I've made the break with my family. I'm waiting here for you."

"Your family will get over it," he says. "Make up a story. Tell them you were fantasizing. Plead temporary insanity. You'll think of something. Nobody else has to know. Ask your family to keep it quiet." I think wildly of Blanche, the blabbermouth.

"How about I tell Floyd to shout it from the roof of his church?" I say bitterly. "How about I take an ad out in the daily paper?"

"Calm down, Jean. You wouldn't want to do any of those things. It would only backfire on you. Think of your reputation. Think how your mother would feel."

"I never heard you concerned about her feelings before this."

"She's a good woman, Jean. Don't put her through any more pain."

"What about *my* pain? You have humiliated me."

"Jean," he says. "I've been thinking. It would be best if we made a clean break of it. I don't want you to come back to the office. I'm letting you go. I'll have your outstanding wages and your severance pay mailed to you tomorrow. I'll write you a letter of reference. I'll write a dozen of them if you want. I'm not worried about you. You're a good assistant. You're young and sharp. You won't have any trouble finding another job. And Jean," he paused, his silence rich with warning, "don't make trouble. Let things go. Forget about it all. Accept it and move on. Don't let yourself get bitter."

In my blouse and skirt, I crawl into bed and sleep all the next day and the next. When I finally get up, snow is falling. It is December, after all. I get undressed, step into the shower and stand there for a good hour, in a hot stream. I put on my housecoat and a pair of thick wool socks and sit at the living-room window for another day, feeling somewhat cleansed from the shower, consuming nothing but ice water, like a nun punishing and purging herself, flushing out bodily poisons.

Outside, big, soft, independent flakes come down. I watch them in all their purity, in all their individuality and separateness, and this seems to give me strength. At first, they melt, these enormous snowflakes, when they touch the ground, and this brings me a sense of effacement, of peace. I feel myself liquefying, dying with them as they fade into the warm gardens, into the grass, still green as summer, fragile vegetation from a gentler season. Gradually, though, they build up, coating lawns, roofs, driveways, like a protective skin, a layer of winter insulation. The apartment is on a wide residential street. From my window, I watch pedestrians tramping over the white, chaste sidewalks, leaving deep footprints in the perfect snow, cars creeping through the white air, crowded buses with wipers, long as a man's arm, beating back and forth. I have the sensation of watching the world from a great, wise height.

Finally, I break my fast, go out and get groceries, carry them back to the apartment. I consume scrambled eggs, Jell-O, stale raisin pie glistening with cornstarch thickener. I have a great deal of time to think.

One afternoon, I compose a letter to Dr. Peter Beveridge.

*Who is the object of your love now? Who? It's not me, we know that, don't we? But who? Is it her? Alice? Alice of the deep dimples? Alice of the naive smile? Is it her? I don't think so. No. I think it's you. You don't love anybody but yourself.*

Into the soft snow I go, with this message, walk through the deep streets with my hand in my pocket, comforted by the sensation of the letter brushing my fingers, by the heat it seems to throw off, as though it were a human organ beating out its irrepressible life. When I reach the dental office, I find myself shaking so badly that I cannot go in. I cannot go in because I am afraid of seeing Dr. Peter Beveridge, afraid of what I already know: that I had never had any power in our relationship. That he had created me as the object of his desire and it had always been within his jurisdiction to abolish me.

I walk then to Dr. Beveridge's house and stop before it. Its lawn is now blanketed in snow, its stone pathway cleanly shovelled. A Christmas wreath hangs on the front door. All is peaceful here and good. It is four o'clock, nearly nightfall. There are lights burning in the house. I stand in the street and watch figures moving in the kitchen behind the drawn curtains. Now I long not to deliver the letter, but simply to go inside and sit down in the welcoming kitchen with Mrs. Dr. Peter Beveridge, to be warmed just a little by her gentle happiness.

A few days later, on one of my afternoon walks, I find myself not far from my apartment, picking my way down a small slope to the Lion's Pool, which is closed, of course, for the winter. Snow is falling in the pool where as children Floyd and I once swam and dove together into the blue water, shrieking. All the children shouting, their sharp, happy cries ringing against the low yellow brick wall. My nostrils flare with the remembered scent of chlorine and of the mildewed change rooms.

On the bleachers too, snow is falling, where in summer there were always a few parents scattered behind a high wire fence, waiting patiently for their children to tire and go home. Among them Mother once sat, her face bent to her book, in the days long ago when she could read fine print. Now, at seventy-five, she has only peripheral vision. There is a big black hole in the centre of everything she looks at. I have begun to think that this condition has affected her intellectual perceptions. She doesn't see the centre of things. She doesn't see the issues, only the complications surrounding them.

I think about how, all these adult years, I have come in the front door after work to find Mother sitting at the kitchen table with her hands lightly folded on her lap, waiting patiently for me to return, her face full of calmness and hope. Just from her pose, I knew that she thought about me all day long. She never left the house, but moved from room to room, dressing slowly, gazing out the windows, picking up her novel, in which she progressed slowly, sometimes reading the same page over and over again, forgetting she'd seen it before, glancing now and then at the clock, thinking: Jean will be having lunch now. Jean will be cleaning up. Jean will be home in an hour. I remember how her tranquillity, her vigilance, used to sustain me.

One day I call home.

"Winter is here again, Mother," I say.

"Hello, Jean," she says. "Yes, I know."

"Dr. Beveridge never left his wife," I tell her.

"I wondered," she says. "I suppose sometimes they don't."

"I have to find another job, Mother."

"That's fine, Jean. You'll find one. Don't worry about that."

"I never meant what I said," I tell her, "about paying the bills. You know I like living with you."

"I know you didn't," she says, and begins to cry. "I'm just so happy to hear your voice," she says, choking on her tears.

"You knew about Dr. Beveridge and me, didn't you?" I say.

"No. I didn't know," she says, clearing her throat. I sense her collecting her defences. Her voice is cautious, innocent. "How would I know?"

"You knew, Mother. You knew and you never said anything. I know you knew. I need you to come clean. I can't return home unless you admit it."

"Yes, I knew," she says reluctantly. "It upset me but I could see it was helping you. You aren't a happy person, Jean."

For a moment neither of us speaks. We listen patiently to the silence, are comforted by it. I can feel her physical presence at the other end of the line.

"Mother?" I finally say.

"Yes?"

"Why aren't you angry with Father?"

She says, "He must have had his reasons for leaving, Jean, and some day he'll come home and explain them to me."

———————

I won't be so rash as to say I miss Floyd and Blanche during the few weeks I live in the apartment. But when I move home I find them easier to accept. I seem to have a finer appreciation for their eccentricities and even catch myself anticipating the sound of their arrival at dinnertime or on the weekends, though I would never admit it to Mother. At Christmas, Floyd says, "Jean, come with us to church, just this once," and I do. Then it becomes a habit. What else is there to do with Sunday mornings? I learn to pray and I learn to forgive. I forgive Father for not taking us to Florida with him and I forgive Dr. Peter Beveridge for choosing to live on with his good wife Alice and his two precocious squash-headed boys in the tranquil bungalow on the nice curved street.

On Sunday mornings, we return from church in Floyd's car,

Mother and I sitting in the back, Blanche in the front, flowing softly across the bench seat.

Blanche tells us piously, "I prayed for Father this morning."

"I prayed for Jean," says Floyd.

"I prayed that Floyd will be sent to the African missions, where he'll be eaten by cannibals," I say.

"Oh, Jean," says Mother, shocked and amused, "you don't mean that!"

"Of course I do."

"Are there still cannibals in Africa, do you suppose?" asks Mother, looking contentedly out the window at the winter trees slipping by like a black screen.

"I hope so," I answer.

# MEMORABILIA

I T WAS LATE on a December afternoon when Loretto spotted
Bev through her living-room window, running down the hill
toward Loretto's house. She could just see Bev's head and her
meagre shoulders bobbing along above the snowbank before she
turned into Loretto's drive, coatless, though it was fifteen below.
Loretto went and opened the door.

"Jesus God, Bev!" she said. "One of these days somebody driving along here will take you for a madwoman and carry you off to
the loony bin!"

Bev ignored the remark. Easing off her boots, she hissed, "You're
not going to believe what I heard in town today!" Her big blue eyes
were shining with excitement, her expression smug, triumphant as
she went into the kitchen and sat down. Loretto followed her cautiously. She didn't like Bev particularly, but she needed her because
it got lonely out here. There were only their two houses on this
stretch of highway just outside the town limits. The road sloped up-
hill from here, and at the top there were large homes with a picturesque view of the town lying in the valley but there was no view
to speak of down here where they were, unless you counted the thin
birch wood across the highway. The railway line ran close behind
their houses.

Occasionally Loretto needed Bev's company. Bev's company was
sometimes—*sometimes*—better than nothing. Her visits supplied

69

Loretto with something to tell Dewey about at night. Bev got into town more than Loretto, who kept to herself mostly, distrusting the gossip, the viciousness of the town. She said the town was too crowded, she didn't like people bumping into her, it was unnatural for people to live on top of each other like that. In contrast, Bev drove into town nearly every day to shop, taking her two kids with her, taking them, for instance, into the lingerie section of Booth's department store where, once, while she was in the change room, the little boy, David, pulled down the underpants on all the mannequins, causing the old woman at the cash to faint. When she came out of the cubicle with her hands full of lacy brassières, Bev laughed. She didn't care. She liked to shock. She liked to leave an impression. Bev heard things in town. She had a way of pulling information out of people she hardly knew, a way of digging and undermining. She was subversive, Loretto thought.

"How about some coffee?" Bev said in the kitchen. "And you're going to need some too. A hot, soothing drink. I hope you're feeling hearty today," she said with exaggerated concern. "I hope you're up to strong news." Her pink lipstick was like paraffin, there was a general waxiness about her complexion, reminding Loretto of a corpse. Bev had the figure of a young teenager because she starved herself or puked up everything she ate until her pelvis bones jutted through her clothes, two curved blades. Her high breasts were the size of muffins, fresh and tempting. Loretto, looking at Bev's bleached hair teased into a brittle, dated flip, thought of a photograph in an old high school yearbook.

"What are you talking about?" demanded Loretto, irritated.

"You better sit down. What I'm going to tell you will knock you flat."

"If it's going to knock me flat," said Loretto, planting her feet solidly on the floor and crossing her arms over her chest, "it won't make any difference if I'm standing or sitting."

"Okay," began Bev with visible relish. "Dewey gets an hour

break at noon, right? He has off from eleven forty-five to twelve forty-five. What does he do with his time?"

"He eats his lunch. I make it for him myself."

"How long do you think it takes him to eat a sandwich? Where do you think he goes after that? Do you suppose he stays at the factory the whole time? Do you think he goes out for fresh air? For a little drive around town, maybe? What do you think he does?"

"Maybe he goes for a drive. I never asked him. Why should that concern me?"

"Think, Loretto. How long would a spin around town every day keep a man like Dewey happy? How long would it be before he got bored? What would he start doing next? Maybe stop in somewheres for a visit? Strike up new acquaintances?"

"I don't know and I don't care. That's his business."

"Oh, but you *should* care, Loretto," crooned Bev with pleasure. "You should make it your business. You'd find yourself surprised."

—————————

The next morning around nine o'clock, Loretto drove into town, parked in front of the paint and wallpaper store on Main Street and went inside. It was a large new store with immense windows facing the street. Loretto had never been in there before. She was the first customer of the day. The girl was there, at the back, organizing the cash and eating a doughnut and coffee, her breakfast. She wore mauve lipstick, heavily applied, and she had a flat chest and the slender legs, hips and behind of a young boy. Her frizzy brown hair hung down on her shoulders. She'd come into work with it still damp. She was seventeen or eighteen.

Unbuttoning her coat, Loretto sat on a stool at one of the high counters near the front where all the wallpaper books were kept. She began to look through one. Soon the girl came along, carrying a large cardboard box. She tore it open and began to unpack rolls of wallpaper, placing them in a bin fixed to the wall.

"Excuse me," Loretto said. The girl straightened up and looked at her with a flat, vacuous face. When she got a better look at Loretto, something flickered across her expression, like a shadow passing over it, a moment of recognition.

"Excuse me, but do we know each other?" Loretto said with patient curiosity.

"I don't think so," the girl lied.

"I feel like we do," said Loretto calmly. "Why is that?"

"I don't know," said the girl, blushing and backing away.

"Are you sure?" Loretto went on in a quiet, reasonable tone. "Perhaps we haven't met directly, but are you certain there isn't some connection? Some link we aren't thinking of? Maybe a person we both know, however distantly or—intimately?"

"I don't know what you're talking about," said the girl, a blend of defiance and fear in her voice.

"No? I wonder."

The girl picked up the empty box and hurried away, pretended to busy herself at the desk. Now Loretto was openly watching her and this was upsetting the girl—Loretto could see this.

Presently, Loretto called back to the girl, "Excuse me. Could you come up here, please? I need some advice." Putting down her papers, the girl reluctantly approached Loretto. "Could you give me your opinion here?" asked Loretto, indicating a wallpaper sample. "Do you like this paper? Do you think it's appropriate for a bedroom? Do you think it would create the right mood?" She was watching the girl's face, which was stricken with alarm. "Do you think it would increase my husband's desire for me? You look like a girl who knows a lot about a man's desire. Especially a married man's." The girl turned and fled to the storage room, her hair flying back, her heels clattering across the linoleum floor. Loretto heard voices back there, a distant door slamming.

Calmly, she continued to turn the big pages of the book, though her own heart was pounding with the raw and brutal excitement of a dog following a scent, certain of its prey. In no hurry to leave, Loretto ran her hand appreciatively over the flocked paper. The store was bright, warm and pleasant and Loretto found it soothing to sit here and watch the traffic slide past the big windows. Women out on a Friday morning shopping for the weekend. A sense of well-being and industry to the town on a day like this. The sun shone, the streets glistened with runoff. An unexpected thaw.

Soon, an older woman, the store manager or owner, emerged from the back room, strapped a gallon of paint onto a machine and flicked a switch, setting the can gyrating. She noticed Loretto looking at her and came to the front of the store.

"May I be of any assistance?" she asked.

"I was dealing with that young girl," said Loretto.

"Wanda." The woman was tiny, withered and bitter-looking as an old dried-up walnut, her hair a thin pink cloud. "She's gone home."

"Oh?" said Loretto with concern. "What's the matter with her?"

"She's feeling sick."

"Oh, dear," said Loretto tragically. "She didn't look too good, did she? She was looking a little peaked. The poor girl. I hope she'll be all right."

"Is there something I can help you with?" asked the woman, growing a little suspicious, impatient with Loretto's solicitude. Perhaps she'd overdone it.

"No," Loretto answered, sliding off the stool and picking up her gloves and purse. "I think I've accomplished what I wanted. Goodbye."

Outdoors in the warm sunshine, Loretto walked along the slushy sidewalk a block or so to the butcher shop, where she pushed through the glass door and shuffled along in line with the other customers until her turn came.

"I'd like five pounds of liver," she told the butcher. "Make it good and bloody."

"Big fry-up tonight, ma'am?" asked the butcher in a friendly way.

"Something like that," said Loretto. She paid for the liver and left the store, carrying back to the car the neat, heavy package wrapped in stiff brown paper and tied with a string. She drove away, turning at the post office, heading north from the commercial street into a residential neighbourhood of old brick homes, some large, some small. Sunshine flooded through the windows, heating the car. Loretto drove along, humming to herself, contentedly stroking the fat butcher's package on the seat beside her, as though it were a purring cat. She drove slowly, enjoying the sight of the red-brick homes against the bright snow and reading the signs. Ottawa Street. Burwash Street. John Street. Soon she came to a short, quiet, wooded road, shady with tall blue pines, like a street in a cottage town. Here was the cemetery, with its stone pillars, its iron gates standing open, its gravestones descending the white hilly terrain sloping down to the river. Next to the cemetery was the place Loretto was looking for, a narrow red-brick house with plain windows, a shallow porch with the Christmas lights still strung along it, a Victorian gable in need of a coat of paint.

With the car idling at the curb, she went up to the house, bearing the package. There was a wicker basket hooked beside the door for a mailbox. Loretto untied the string on the package, opened the butcher's paper and dumped the liver into the basket, in among some letters left by the postman. By the time she was back in her car, the dark blood was flowing out the basket, trickling down the side of the house. As she drove away, she saw the girl, Wanda, standing in an upstairs window, holding a white curtain aside, watching her.

———

That night Loretto waited for Dewey to come home and face her. It was well after nine before he arrived. Loretto knew why he was late. Bev had called earlier.

"I heard the girl tried to kill herself," Bev told Loretto. "Dewey was called away from the factory. The police came and picked him up and took him to the hospital so he could talk to the doctors. Talk to the girl. Maybe try and calm her down."

Loretto was sitting at the kitchen table with a cup of coffee when Dewey got home. He came and stood in the kitchen doorway, filling it with his bulk. He was a tall, heavyset man with a sandy brush-cut and long, lustrous eyelashes.

"It's finished," Loretto told him. By that, she meant: Don't ever see her again. If you try to, I'm warning you I can't be held responsible for what I might do. We won't speak of it again. We'll go back to Life before Wanda.

"I know it's finished!" Dewey said angrily. "You made goddamn sure of that, didn't you?"

"What did you expect me to do? Write her a thank-you note?"

"No, I didn't expect that. Not from *you*."

"Do you know how humiliating it was for me to have to face her?"

"You didn't have to face her. You didn't have to go into that store."

"I like to meet things head-on."

"Why did you have to go for her? Why did you go and scare the shit out of the kid? You could have kept it between you and me."

"And pretend she was just an innocent bystander? I believe in people taking the consequences of their actions."

"What you did might have killed her. How would you have felt then?"

"The slashes on her wrists weren't sincere," Loretto scoffed. "She called the ambulance herself before she'd bled a thimbleful."

Dewey turned from her in disgust and walked away. "Why did

you do it?" Loretto yelled after him. "Why would you be attracted to someone like her? How could you touch her pathetic body? I've seen more flesh on an insect! I've seen more intelligence on the face of a moron! She isn't even worth talking about. She's *nothing*!"

———————

"Maybe you went too far," Bev said to Loretto the next day on the phone.

"She had it coming to her."

"She was just a child," Bev pointed out.

"She was old enough to commit adultery."

"They don't call it that any more."

"What do they call it?"

"A love affair."

"*Love*!" Loretto spat out.

Wanda's parents were contacted by the police and called home. All the way from Florida, where they spent their winters, summoned from their comfortable trailer home at considerable expense, flying because of the emergency when ordinarily they would have returned economically by car in May. Called back to the Canadian winter because of a package of liver.

"They didn't have to come back because of a package of liver," Loretto told Bev. "They had to come back because their daughter is a slut. It's time they knew what she was up to. Using their house for her carryings on. How many other men were there before Dewey?"

The whole affair caught the imagination of the town. People visited the wallpaper store to talk to the pink-haired lady—Florence Quickly was her name—asking exactly what Loretto had said to the girl, asking if Loretto had purchased any wallpaper in the end. They'd dropped in at the butcher shop. How much liver had Loretto bought, they wanted to know, and at what price per pound? The butcher offered a week-long special on liver to take advantage of the publicity. He was sold out every day. Households all over town were eating it. People drove past the girl's house to look at the blood stain, dark as tanned leather and frozen to the front of the house. Wanda's mother was seen by some spectators on her knees on the front porch with her Florida tan and a pail of steaming water, trying to scrub off the liver blood with a stiff brush.

"She's lucky I didn't smear blood all over the front door, like they did in the Bible," Loretto told Bev.

"You probably would have, if you'd thought of it. The Angel of Death. What would you do," Bev asked Loretto, "what would you do if Dewey ran around again?"

"He wouldn't dare."

"But if he did. I mean, the liver. That's a tough act to follow. What would you do next time?"

"Something drastic."

"Murder?"

"Murder would be too kind."

Loretto referred to the girl as "Wanda the Wallflower." Dewey had not seen Wanda the Wallflower since the day Loretto dropped the liver off. Wanda the Wallflower was permanently out of the picture now. After she was discharged from the hospital, her parents took her back to Florida with them, to recuperate. In the spring, she would return to Canada and move to a nearby city, where she would enroll in a community college, intending to become an interior decorator.

"That'll get her into a lot of bedrooms," mused Loretto.

---

Early in January, Dewey came home after work with an armload of textbooks.

"What are those for?" asked Loretto, looking up from the television set.

"I have to study for an exam," Dewey told her. "I've decided to become a policeman." He'd been so impressed with the policemen who'd picked him up that day at the factory and taken him over to the hospital to see Wanda: their professionalism, their sympathy for his awkward predicament, their quiet respect. It had made him stop and think. Now he knew he wanted to help people, as those officers had helped him. Loretto was not happy at being reminded of Wanda.

"You'll have to lose weight first," she told Dewey. "They don't let fat men be cops." He reddened but didn't answer her. He went to the kitchen table, sat down and opened a thick volume. "You could have consulted me first," she said in a conciliatory tone, though she thought to herself that she'd seen some kind of dramatic change coming. Since the incident with Wanda, Dewey had been uncharacteristically quiet. No more jokes. No more clowning around. He'd stopped drinking. Now he started to cut back on meals. He shed pounds. On the weekends, he went jogging out on the highway, running clear to the next town and back.

Sometimes this new, reflective, philosophical Dewey made Loretto nervous. Other times she was content to think that this was all part of a general renovation, a self-improvement regimen Dewey had undertaken, having recognized his own folly. He'd seen the error of his ways, had set his course on the straight and narrow. Every evening after coming home from the factory, he opened his textbooks, made notes, memorized, tested himself. In February he passed the entrance exam to the police academy. Gradually Loretto grew used to the idea of Dewey in a policeman's uniform. *My husband is a law enforcement officer*, she imagined herself saying to people sometime in the future.

One evening, Dewey said, "Loretto, maybe we should think about moving into town." He and Loretto had grown up on adjacent tobacco farms. At eighteen, they'd eloped without two cents between them and moved here, to the edge of town, because the rent was cheap and because Loretto had not been quite ready to re-linquish the country. She was not sure she was city material. There were a lot of people she didn't like.

"We need to become part of a community," Dewey told her.

"Don't you think you've done enough already to fit in?" Loretto asked sarcastically, thinking of Wanda the Wallflower. Dewey shook his head in frustration and went back to his reading. "Why would we want to fit into the town?" Loretto continued. "So we can be like them? Sleep around and not have any conscience? I don't want any part of it."

Then Dewey told her she was too critical, she should try to accept people for what they were, stop expecting them to be perfect or make the kinds of choices she made. This was his new posture, this liberalism, now that he was studying to become a law enforcement officer.

"What are you training for, anyway?" Loretto asked him. "To be a cop, or a psychologist?"

"You're afraid of people, Loretto," said Dewey.

"Fat chance."

"You're afraid of yourself."

———————

One afternoon, Bev herded her kids down the snowy highway to Loretto's place. Loretto had reluctantly agreed to babysit them. Bev pushed the kids into the house. "I won't be long," she said.

"Oh, I bet," said Loretto knowingly.

Bev was wearing a low-cut black top with her boobs popping out of it, a black miniskirt, a big shiny red belt, red spike heels, a short raccoon jacket Gabriel gave her for Christmas. She ran out in the snow in her high heels. Just then a long black car came along. It stopped and she got in. It was four thirty before she returned.

"I don't know why Gabriel isn't good enough for you," Loretto told Bev in the kitchen. "I think he's a peach." Gabriel was Bev's husband, a cabdriver. He owned his own car, something Bev was always quick to point out. It helped Bev to accept that Gabriel was just a taxi driver and not some rich business executive. Owning his own car made him something like an entrepreneur.

"Peaches are boring," answered Bev. "Peaches are bland. Peaches go soft and pulpy after a while."

Loretto said she didn't know why Bev needed another man at all.

"*Man*!" said Bev ironically. "You mean *men*!"

"What are you smirking at?" said Loretto.

"You don't want to know."

"No, I don't," agreed Loretto, "but tell me anyway."

Loretto had already heard about the salesman who came to Bev's house in a refrigerated truck selling fancy dinners, gourmet meals all made up and ready to pop into the oven after a strenuous day of bridge or shopping. He carried in boxes of these meals and stacked them on Bev's kitchen table. Bev couldn't stop him. Or wouldn't. Chicken Kiev. Beef Wellington. Tournedos Rossini. Lobster Thermidor. Coquilles St. Jacques. He was from Newfoundland, a young fellow with a rich, beautiful Newfie accent, the words rolling off his tongue thick as slices of bread. He had a friend with him. They stood in Bev's kitchen. The salesman told her he could win a trip to Florida if Bev placed a big order. All he needed was one more big order. She couldn't resist. She couldn't stop looking at his tanned face, his dimples, his dark shiny hair. She wrote a cheque for two hundred dollars worth of food. She told the young man she hoped she would see him again. The next day he came back without his friend. She put the kids in front of the television and went for a drive in the country.

"It was just a little ride. It was harmless," she'd told Loretto.

"Sure it was."

Then there was the company president. He was the kinkiest. He drove her into the country. It was always the country. What Bev and her lovers had put the countryside through was pretty shocking. He took a deserted road, then a cow path, made Bev lie down naked on the hood of his car, poured champagne all over her bare breasts, burned her breasts with the tip of his cigar, slapped her mouth so that it bled. This was what Bev lived for. She had to have it.

"But didn't Gabriel ask questions?" said Loretto. "Didn't he see the burns?"

"Gabriel sees what he wants to see."

"What if Gabriel saw you with one of these men? He's driving around out there in his cab."

"We did see him once when we were heading out of town. I ducked down in the car. We were parked right beside him at an intersection. I thought the light would never turn green."

The businessman became violent and serious about Bev. He wanted to marry her but he couldn't.

"Why not?" asked Loretto.

"He's Catholic. The Catholic church frowns on divorce."

"Well, how does it feel about adultery?" asked Loretto.

"You are so jaded," Bev told Loretto sadly. "You judge people too harshly. You don't trust them. You don't give them a chance." Anyway, Bev said, she didn't want to marry anyone else. She liked things this way: the layers of intrigue, the close calls, the double-edged conversations, the prospect of risk. Life wasn't worth living without this. She was smoking a cigarette and her hands, themselves the colour of cigarette ash, were shaking.

"You're sick," Loretto told her. "Jesus God, you're sick!"

"I know," Bev grinned.

When the weather turned cold, the Catholic businessman took Bev to motels. The more sordid the better. The possibility of mice in the corners of the room, of holes in the towels and sheets, of grime and turpitude and destruction drove both of them wild with lust. The businessman chased Bev around the motel room, roaring like a lion. When Bev locked herself in the bathroom, he broke the door down. He tore the shower curtain off its hooks, wrapped her in it and carried her back to the bed.

"That sounds like rape," said Loretto.

"Rape can be fun."

Loretto wasn't sure how much of this to believe. She thought Bev must be making some of it up.

"You bring out the worst in men," she told Bev.

"Sometimes the worst is the best."

"You like the idea of driving a man mad."

"No, I don't."

"Oh, yes you do."

"I like to be desired."

"You look like a sex-craved bitch."

"I *am* a sex-craved bitch."

"And you love every minute of it."

"Maybe."

"Maybe, nothing."

Where did these men come from? How did they find Bev? Loretto thought it must be word of mouth. Loretto had to listen to all of this. Why did she listen to this smut? She didn't know. In one way she was ashamed of herself for listening and in another way it made her feel good. It made her feel she was the only sane person in the world.

———————

One afternoon, deep in March, someone called Loretto and told her what she later supposed she should have been expecting to hear all along. The message was brief but Loretto tried to keep the person on the line as long as she could. She listened to the voice, which was throaty, soft, benevolent, tried to think of who it could be. Many possibilities flashed through her head. Wanda the Wallflower, calling to exact revenge. Wanda's mother, angry about the liver blood.

The desiccated wallpaper lady, Florence Quickly, with her hair like pink candy-floss. The old clerk who had fainted in Booth's lingerie department.

It could have been any of these women but Loretto somehow knew it wasn't. It was a complete stranger calling with a gift and this was the peculiar thing: the news *was* like a gift, something offered free of charge, a piece of information Loretto needed to have and at the same time it was like poison, a poison offering, kind as mercy killing.

Loretto didn't know whether to feel angry or grateful. She did feel exposed, humiliated, foolish to realize that this stranger knew more about her life, about Dewey, than Loretto herself did. The voice cut through Loretto, like a sharp bitter wind sweeping through her body. "Who is this?" demanded Loretto several times. "Who is this?" But what difference did it make who it was? It was the message that was important and Loretto knew instantly that it was true—hadn't she noticed that the pieces of life always seem to fit together in this cruel way? The stranger hung up. Loretto had been upstairs folding the laundry. Outside there was a snowstorm. Large heavy flakes were falling, thick as white paint, coating every-thing, enveloping the house like a muffling shroud, shutting out air. Loretto hung up the phone and stood with her hand on the re-ceiver. The house was silent as the storm. Within the whirling cone of white, Loretto felt her own insignificance.

All afternoon, working around the house, Loretto kept hearing the voice on the phone. Not the words especially, but the texture of it, a kind of remote yet ostentatious concern, possibly sympathy. Which was something Loretto didn't want. Not from a stranger. Not from anybody. But was it sympathy? If that person was so sym-pathetic, why would she even call Loretto? Guile. Phoniness. Mockery.

The next day, Saturday, Loretto and Dewey got up around ten o'clock. Dewey stood at the window and read the thermometer.

"Maybe I shouldn't go jogging today," he said. "It's minus thirty and it looks like there's a wind."

"You better go," Loretto said. "You need the exercise. Just bundle up."

She sat on the living-room couch, watching him put on his wind pants, runners, jacket and wool hat, a pair of thick mittens.

"Don't hurry back," she said. Moving to the window, she watched him run up the hill, jogging on the ploughed highway shoulder. If he did the full run, he'd be gone at least an hour. As soon as he disappeared over the top of the hill, Loretto got to work. She went into the bedroom, opened up the clothes closet, gathered Dewey's shirts into her arms, carried them through the house, opened the front door and threw them out into the snow. Back in the bedroom, she collected his socks, underwear, slacks, jackets, ties and threw them outdoors too. She'd made several trips before the phone rang. It was Bev.

"What's going on over there, Loretto?" she asked. "What the heck are you doing?"

"Oh, I just thought I'd air out Dewey's clothes," Loretto told her.

There was a pause. "What's the matter, Loretto? You sound angry." Bev's voice was quiet, worried, scared.

"You tell me! You tell me why I'm angry! You seem to know more about what's going on in my life than I do!"

Another long pause. "It was only once, Loretto."

"Once! That's not what I heard. Once what? Once a week? Once a day? I suppose I was babysitting your brats at the time!"

"They're not brats, Loretto. They're nice children. Loretto, don't do something rash."

"Why not? Why do I have to always be the reasonable one?"

"You're not reasonable, Loretto. You're rigid. You drive people away with your perfectionism. People are human, Loretto."

"Don't tell me what people are! I can see it for myself!"

"You're not an easy person to live with. Any man would have done what Dewey did." Bev's tone was calm, reasonable, patronizing. Loretto couldn't stand it.

"Shut up!" she shouted. "Shut your cheap face!" She hung up the phone and returned to her task. She went around the house, opening cupboards, opening drawers, collecting everything she could find of Dewey's and throwing it outside. Toothbrush, shaving kit, shoe shine kit, hairbrush, deodorant, aftershave, soap-on-a-rope, throat lozenges, Swiss Army knife, brass shoehorn, cuff links, battery charger, alarm clock radio, stamp collection, baseball glove, baseball cap, baseball uniform, curling shoes, fishing rod and tackle, squash racket, ice skates, hockey stick, hockey puck, compass, walkman, textbooks and notepaper, pocketknife, pocket calculator, paperback novels, high school pennant, high school graduation photograph, framed photograph of his mother, coffee mug, favourite cereal, favourite cookies, auto and sports magazines, umbrella, wristwatch, camera, birth certificate, piggy bank, overcoat, galoshes, rubbers, rain slicker, records, sunglasses, jockstrap. By the end of the hour she'd torn apart every room in the house. The process left her feeling amplified, light-headed, dizzyingly objective, as though she were on some powerful drug, as though her body carried all this out automatically, without instructions from her brain.

She went outside and locked the car, came back in, locked the front and back doors and all the windows. Then she stood in the living room watching for Dewey. She wanted to see the expression on his face. That was what she wanted more than anything right now. Soon he appeared over the hill, jogging at a steady pace, his head down. A moment later he caught sight of the house. He slowed down, stopped, then started up again, running faster than before. By this time the wind had carried some things off the lawn. Shirts and ties had blown out onto the highway. Magazines, study notes were over in the woods, snagged on branches. He stopped and picked up a tie from the road, looked at it dumbly like he was trying to read some difficult instructions written on it. His face was red from the wind. He waded through the deep snow to where Loretto was standing at the window.

"Loretto, what the hell is this?" he shouted.

"You think!" Loretto called through the window. "You think and maybe you'll figure out what it's about!"

He went to the front door and tried it, then went back down onto the lawn and stood at the window again.

"Loretto, unlock the door! Jesus Christ, Loretto, I'm freezing my goddamn ass off out here!" His face was turning blue. She could see he was shivering. She hoped he'd get hypothermia.

"I'm glad," she shouted. "That makes me happy! Because it's just what you deserve!"

He looked around, incredulous, his hands on his hips. "Fuck!" he said, and kicked the snow.

"Bingo!" Loretto called through the window. "You guessed it. That's what this is all about! It's about fucking!"

Loretto went into the bathroom and sat on the edge of the tub. She heard Dewey at the back door, at the windows. She was afraid he might break one of them and get in that way. Her whole body was shaking. She bit hard on a knuckle to steady herself and tasted blood. Soon the sound of Dewey looking for a point of entry ceased. Returning to the living room, she saw him wading through the snow, gathering up whatever he could hold. Cars were passing on the highway, slowing down, driving over the things on the road. Some of them honked cheerfully. With his arms full, Dewey walked up the highway toward Bev's house.

———————

In the spring Loretto had to look at the things Dewey didn't collect. The cereal and cookies, for instance, he left. The squirrels got those but the boxes remained. Other small heavy objects that had slipped down through the snow: engraved fountain pen, nail clipper, penknife, key chain, pinkie ring, wedding ring. In the spring the snow melted, revealing these memorabilia. By this time, though, Loretto was packing her bags. She'd found another place to live. She carried her things out to the car, tramping on the rings, the fountain pen, grinding them with pleasure into the moist heaving earth.

Loretto moved into town. She got a job as a dispatcher for the taxi company. Its offices were just off Princess Street, behind the movie theatre, in a corner of the bus depot. It was busy there, with people arriving and departing all the time on the big wheezing Greyhound buses. From her corner desk, Loretto spoke into a microphone to the drivers out in their cars. She was the only woman employed by the taxi company. The owner said the drivers liked the domestic sound of a woman's voice coming to them over their two-way radios.

It was a pig sty in the office, at the desk where Loretto sat, where other dispatchers sat on other shifts. Grease and dust, cigar butts, cigarette ash. The filth reminded her of the farm. At first she tried to clean it up but gradually she got used to it. It wasn't until she went home at night that she noticed the dirt under her own fingernails, the smell of cigar smoke on her clothes, in her hair. It formed a greasy film on her skin, like cooking fumes settling on a stove hood.

People got used to seeing Loretto there, speaking into her microphone, looking out the window at Fink's Hair Salon across the way. They waved at her when they passed by. People got to know her and they didn't get to know her. Once a month Bev's ex-husband, Gabriel, came into the office to collect his paycheque. He wouldn't look at Loretto. When she contacted him over the radio, they talked to each other in a cold impersonal way as if they'd never been neighbours. Loretto guessed that Gabriel was angry with her for pushing things. If she hadn't pushed things, he and Bev could have kept going along as they had been, and what was the matter with that?

Loretto had begun to think she took too straightforward an

approach to life, that she saw things too much in the black and white. The truth was that life used to make Loretto sick. The way people carried on. But what was the harm in what Bev and Dewey had done? If everybody was still happy while it was going on, what was the harm? What people didn't know wouldn't hurt them. Maybe running around didn't mean anything at all. It was all just surface stuff. Games. Perks. Little indulgences. Little white sins. Maybe a person had a right to them. Maybe life demanded it. Maybe there was no right or wrong. That's what Bev used to say.

Dewey changed. At least, Loretto heard he did. He became even slimmer, developed grey hair at his temples. She heard he was gentler and wiser now, nicer and more settled. Why couldn't he have got that way sooner? He was admired and well liked in town as an honest, moderate police officer on his way up through the force. People seemed to have forgotten about the two affairs he'd had, but of course they hadn't forgotten about the liver. Of course not. That story had passed into legend. At first it seemed incredible to Loretto that Dewey could command such respect in the community after the way he acted. He wasn't fit to wear the uniform, as far as she was concerned. He made a joke out of the law. But as time passed, her thoughts on the subject changed.

Now and again Loretto dreamed a dream about Dewey, and in it she was trying to help him pick up his clothes out of the snow and carry them back into the house. Loretto wondered if she was capable any more of throwing someone out in the snow. She wondered if she was still the same person who'd done that five years before. She hoped not. She couldn't say why. She couldn't say what it was she hoped she'd acquired. Tolerance, patience, forbearance, mercy. Or, on the other hand, pride, dignity, imperviousness. The ability to rise above the smallness of others.

After the discovery of the affair between Bev and Dewey, Bev and Gabriel had stayed together for a while. But eventually Bev ran off, leaving Gabriel with the kids. Five years after Loretto and

Dewey split up, Dewey got married to the town librarian. She was eight years older than he was and she had blonde hair falling in a classic page boy to her shoulders. When she heard about the marriage, Loretto went to the public library on a Saturday morning. She wanted to understand. She climbed the porch steps and passed between the fat, leafy columns into the pink sandstone building. She sat down in a window corner in the periodical section at a scarred mahogany table as big as a bed, within earshot of the circulation desk. She thought if she sat there long enough listening to this librarian talking on the phone, talking to the library patrons about their overdue books, their books on reserve, that she might begin to understand how a chic, educated woman like this could love Dewey. How they fit together. It was disturbing.

She sat there for several hours in the brilliant sunshine, looking out the big windows at an empty school yard, at the dry, dusty, bleached streets, at petunias spilling from flower boxes in front of the Public Utilities building. She sat there with old liver-spotted men who read newspapers or dozed off with spittle foaming in the corners of their mouths. She listened to the librarian's knifelike voice and still she did not understand. She did not understand but she could not make herself get up and leave. She felt sapped by the hot sunshine, weighed down by the thick dark table, by the stacks of brittle and yellowing newspapers, by the cumulative ages of these dry men with their papery skins.

She listened to them snoring and to the noise of the photocopier whirring somewhere in the stacks until the librarian went out for lunch. Loretto heard her giving instructions to someone, a young assistant, and the sound of her heels clicking across the floor, ringing up into the pink dome, clattering down the stairs to the front door, which swung open, letting the din of the street traffic spill in. Only then could Loretto force her legs to move, swing them around slowly, slide off the chair, walk like a zombie to the front door and out into the yellow summer heat.

89

The librarian had some money. She owned a house she'd inherited from her father. It was on a private peninsula with such a narrow neck that it was almost like an island sitting out in the wide river. Loretto had always wanted to live on an island. The big white house was visible from the bridge. Loretto sometimes drove across the bridge and saw it there among the trees, saw the stony bank and acres of mown grass. Sometimes she slowed down to get a better look at it, but invariably a car behind her would honk and she'd have to move on.

At the taxi office, Loretto watched the travellers' comings and goings. She looked out the window at the bright, windblown street. Sometimes she wondered about Bev, pictured her riding in a spacious car somewhere, floating over country roads with a strange and attractive man. Enjoying life. Doing what she pleased. Seeking moments of brief but intense happiness, moments of splendour. At times, Loretto felt a desire, a powerful need, to communicate with Bev, though of course this was impossible. No one knew where she was. Nevertheless, one summer afternoon during a quiet moment on the desk, Loretto drew a piece of stationery out of the drawer and picked up a pen. *Dear Bev,* she wrote.

# SUMMER SKY: WHITE SHIP

## I

ON Saturdays and Sundays, as soon as the clock reads twelve noon, the Kings begin to drink. Eric King, opening a beer in the kitchen, says to Anne, "You're fat." Anne wears a bikini and measures forty inches around the waist.

"You wanted babies," she says grimly, slapping cheese sandwiches together for the children, "so now you have a fat wife." To console himself, Eric slips a hand inside the seat of her bikini.

"Get lost," she says. "The children will see."

"They wouldn't know the difference," says Eric.

"They've got eyes. Anyway, this is my week off."

Eric glances at the calendar, suspicious. He can't keep track of Anne's cycle. "You said you had the curse *last* week," he says resentfully.

The Kings' three children—all girls—are under the age of eight. Eric, aiming for a son, wanted at least one more child, but after an ectopic pregnancy, the doctor said another try might kill Anne. Eric thought it was worth the risk but finally gave in. "Well, all right," he said grudgingly. "No more kids."

Eric's concession to Anne for having the children in the first

91

place was to let her name them. She has called them Jade and Desiré and Cassandra. After Eric has had a few beers, he gets the children's names mixed up. He calls Jade Cassandra and Cassandra Desiré and Desiré Jade. It's not that he doesn't love them, he says, only that he can't remember which is which.

"How can you do that?" says Anne. "How can you confuse your own children?" She appears amused, but is not. The only time she smiles at Eric any more is when she's mad at him. "If they were boys, you wouldn't forget their names," she says.

Eric, reclining in swim trunks in a deck chair, scratches the hair on his stomach. "Jesus Christ," he says stoically, and blows cigarette smoke out his nostrils. He is still slight and wiry, though there has been a perceptible slackening of his stomach and chest muscles. His reddish hair, which he grows long in the summer, the way he wore it when he met Anne ten years ago, hangs in his eyes.

"Get a haircut," Anne has told him.

"I look younger this way."

"What you look like is an old fool."

The Kings have a waterfront property where the river measures a mile wide. A lawn slopes down from the white bungalow to the water's edge. Here, there is a narrow beach and a cedar deck with benches and wooden barrels full of petunias. The Kings' place is too large to be a cottage and too small to be a house. Because the river at this point is warm and shallow, there is a constant stream of summer visitors, mostly Eric's family. The place has, in fact, become a halfway house for Eric's no-good brothers, Lance and Reed.

This very minute, down on the lawn, the children are climbing up on Lance. They love his white, fat stomach. Lance is big and slow, with an army haircut. Months ago, when trying to kill himself with a pistol, he succeeded only in inflicting a minor shoulder wound, though he did scare himself half to death. This morning, after Lance arrived, Anne searched through his duffle bag while he was outside to see if he had brought a firearm. She imagines him going on a shooting spree here, some sunny afternoon, leaving the beach littered with beer bottles and dead bodies. She also went into the master bedroom and checked to make sure the gun cabinet was locked. Eric began to collect guns when Anne stopped wanting to have sex. Yesterday, at breakfast, Eric said to her, "If there's ever a nuclear war, I'm going to shoot you and the children and myself."

"I'd rather have a bomb dropped on me than to get shot by you," said Anne, her mouth full of toast. "You're a lunatic. Sometimes it scares me to think who I'm living with."

Anne cannot really object to Lance, because he is cheerful and is building a treehouse for the girls. It is slender Reed, with his tight jeans and his thick auburn hair, that she must be careful of. The last time he visited, he kissed her in the garage while everyone else was down swimming. Then he persuaded her to give him a twenty-four-hour loan of two hundred dollars and skipped the province for a month. Before leaving, Reed said to Eric, "That Anne's a hot little bundle, isn't she?" They were up in the loft of the workshop Eric had built behind the house. He was ambitious around the property, and creative with a hammer and saw.

"Have you had your fucking hands on her?" Eric shouted, rising from the plumbing he was putting in. "I'll break your fucking neck!" he warned, throwing a punch at Reed.

After Reed roared off in his Jeep, Eric went looking for Anne and found her in the laundry room, folding diapers. "Have you been coming on to Reed?" he asked her.

Anne snorted. "I messed up my life badly enough marrying *you*. Why would I want to get involved with one of your dumb brothers?"

A couple of days later, when Anne finally figured out that Reed had taken her for a ride, she went down to the water's edge while Eric was at work and threw her wallet far out into the river. "It was stolen in town," she said to him that night. "It had the grocery money in it."

"I bust my ass to earn a dollar and you go and throw it away!" he shouted.

"I *told* you it was stolen," Anne repeated quietly. She was kneeling beside the tub, running the bathwater for the children, her back to Eric. She didn't want him to see her face. She didn't care about the money. Two hundred dollars thrown away didn't make her any more miserable than she already was. Listening to Eric rage, she might even have been strangely happy the money was gone, she might have been amused by Eric's anger. It gave her a twisted pleasure to see him stiffed out of two hundred bucks by his own brother. He had it coming to him, for inviting Reed up here all the time to take advantage of them, for being such a son of a bitch himself.

That night in bed, staring up at the ceiling, she said, "I don't recognize myself any more."

"I don't recognize you either," said Eric. "You used to have a waistline."

"I mean, I have no convictions about anything any more. Things used to seem so important. All my values are slipping away."

"What values?" asked Eric, the glowing tip of his cigarette floating like a red star in the dark room. "I don't remember you ever having any."

"When I met you I was a nice girl. I'd never sworn or told a lie or got drunk in my life."

"If you were so much better, why did you marry me, then?"

Anne had to think for a moment. "Because you were wild and you had a bankroll and black satin sheets on your bed and you knew all about grass. If only I'd listened to Daddy's advice."

"If you think he was some kind of saint, you're kidding yourself," Eric told her. "He ran around on your old lady."

"Bullshit."

"He told me himself."

Eric waited for Anne to rise up from the mattress and pummel

94

him on the chest with her fists, as she'd often done when they were young, when they were still in love, but she lay still.

"I feel sorry for you," she said quietly. "You don't even know any more when you're lying."

———————

Down on the river, Anne's mother-in-law, the original Mrs. King, emerging from the water wearing a purple bathing suit and a gash of red lipstick, peels a bathing cap from her short white hair. She climbs the grass to the deck with the long, mannish stride she developed in the Women's Army Corps thirty years ago. Her broad shoulders and aggressive bosom make it easy to imagine her in a uniform studded with brass buttons. She is capable of giving as crippling a bear hug as any of her sons, and of drinking them under the table. As long as she can remember, they have called her "The Boxer," because of the way she punched them around as children when they stepped out of line. She still terrifies them, but they worship her all the same, as soldiers fear and love their commanding officer. She, in turn, is proud of her boys, whom she raised on her own, after their father drank himself to death. In her wallet she carries baby pictures not of her grandchildren, but of her sons. Of course, she loves her granddaughters too, but thinks it's a shame that Anne had all girls. Mrs. King has driven up for the afternoon, bringing her own bottle of gin, and is threatening to stay the night.

"I didn't bring a suitcase," she bellows. "I'll sleep in the raw." She is what people call a "character," and want to have at their parties, just as they might import a magician or a clown to entertain their guests.

"You wouldn't dare!" says Lance, grinning with admiration. Then he pauses and looks at her. "Would you?" he asks with serious concern.

The long clapboard bungalow used to be Mrs. King's house. Anne and Eric bought it from her, using most of Anne's small inheritance as a down payment. Mrs. King has moved to an apartment in the city where, in the evenings, she weeps and cheats at solitaire. She has got thick in the waist.

The three boys rise to meet her when she comes out of the water. Reed, fresh from a jail term for street-fighting and possession of marijuana, hands her a towel. She takes it from him, then swats him with it, a playful, malicious grin on her face. Reed, in turn, dodges the towel with a graceful swing of his hips, steps across the patio and punches Lance in the shoulder.

Anne, coming down the grassy slope with what she's been able to scavenge from the fridge—dill pickles, some cold chicken she'd forgotten about, the remnants of a jellied salad, potato chips, and the cheese sandwiches for the girls—feels the tray she's carrying begin to shake. Seeing Mrs. King and her sons together, she is trembling all over with the feeling that there is violence simmering just under the surface of things.

As it turns out, Eric, Reed and Lance are not interested right now in food, for Eric has brought his telescope out from the shed and has set it up on the patio. He directs it at a beach down the river where, all weekend long, he and his brothers have been observing the movements of a young girl named Judith.

"Judith babysat for us once," Anne tells them, "and at the end of the evening it took Eric three hours to drive her home."

"I ran out of gas," Eric says.

"Sure you did," says Anne cynically.

"Jesus! Look at those cans!" cries Eric, squinting through the lens.

"Lemme see," says Lance greedily, but Eric will not surrender the telescope.

"That must be against the law," observes Anne flatly. "Invasion of privacy or something."

"There is no law up here," Mrs. King boasts in a proprietary tone, as though she'd invented the river herself. "Never was."

"She's taken her top off," Eric reports, peering through the lens. Lance and Reed grab for the telescope and Reed wins it. He bends, squints through the scope, one eye squeezed shut.

"Liar!" he says to Eric, disappointed.

"Juveniles," Anne observes with disgust, holding the wooden bowl of potato chips, ready to offer them around.

"Oh, be a sport, Anne," says Mrs. King. "Boys will be boys."

The two little girls run up from the water's edge. The older one, Jade, is crying because her younger sister, Desiré, has splashed water in her face. Jade has legs like a sparrow and Anne's straight sandy hair.

"What a sullen little face she has," observes Mrs. King, rubbing at her own arms with a towel. "She didn't get that from *our* side of the family."

"I didn't splash her," says Desiré, crossing her arms stubbornly. Like her father, she is a fluent liar. She refuses a sandwich from the plate.

"We don't know what Desiré lives on," boasts Eric. "She's never hungry." Of all the girls, Desiré would be Eric's pick. He says she's got street smarts, at the age of four.

"If she doesn't want her sandwiches, I'll eat them," offers Lance.

Anne bends over, taking Jade's hand. "Don't cry," she says comfortingly.

"You baby that kid," Eric accuses Anne. "No wonder she's a suck about water. You can't live on a river and be a suck about water."

"It's too cold for her," says Anne. "She's thin-blooded."

"The water is seventy-two degrees, for Chris'sake," says Eric. "I checked the temperature half an hour ago."

"When the boys were young," recalls Mrs. King proudly, a glass of gin in her hand, "they went for a swim every morning, before school. In the month of May. I drove them into the water with a two-by-four. No better way to toughen a kid up. You could hear their howls miles down the river." The boys grin, remembering.

"'S'true," says Lance, a sandwich in each of his big mitts.

Mrs. King puts down her drink, gets up and moves toward Jade. "Here," she says. "Grandma's going to teach you about water." She seizes Jade's wrist. The child, squeezed in beside Anne on a lawn chair, pulls away, grabbing at Anne's leg. She whimpers as Mrs. King yanks her up and leads her across the patio.

"Eric, stop her," says Anne, alarmed, rising from her chair, but Eric holds Anne back, twisting her arm behind her.

"It's only water," he says.

Mrs. King has picked Jade up by both wrists. The child's legs churn the air, her body twists in Mrs. King's iron grip. Her screams carry across the water. Neighbours on nearby beaches rise from their chairs and stare across at the Kings' property, shading their eyes from the sun. Now Mrs. King has waded into the water up to her waist, pulling Jade along beside her.

"Hold your breath," she warns, but Jade, her chin touching the water, is screaming too loud to hear her. Mrs. King dunks her once and Jade comes up choking, spitting water, red in the face. Mrs. King dunks her again.

"Eric, let go!" Anne protests, struggling to free her wrist from his grip. "Mrs. King!" she pleads on Jade's behalf.

"Mom, take it easy," Reed calls out, concerned but respectful. Lance steps forward, nervous. Finally, Mrs. King turns and pulls Jade through the water, back to shore. Jade runs, sobbing, to Anne, who wraps her in a towel and picks her up.

"She's okay, the big baby," says Mrs. King, standing now on the shore, water streaming down her heavy, blue-veined thighs.

"A little water never hurt anyone," agrees Eric.

Anne picks Jade up and carries her across the lawn toward the house. "You're nothing but a pack of thugs!" she calls over her shoulder.

Reed and Lance look at each other a little sheepishly. They like Anne because she's a good cook.

"Anne!" Eric calls after her. "Anne, for Chris'sake!" He turns and looks at the river angrily. "Shit!" he spits out in disgust.

Later, up at the house after Jade has gone down to the beach again, Anne opens a kitchen cupboard and removes a glass. Glancing outside to make sure that nobody is coming, she closes her eyes, raises the glass and smashes it violently on the floor. The shards shoot in every direction, skidding across the linoleum, raining against her bare ankles like needle pricks. The pain and the sight of the shattered glass strengthen her, make her feel purified, purged of her anger. She places her palm flat against her brow, closes her eyes and takes several deep, calming breaths. Then, relaxed, she crosses the room, opens a long cupboard, takes out a broom. She sweeps the glass up into a dustpan and dumps it in the garbage, humming to herself. Sitting down in the living room, she picks up a book.

Soon she sees Eric coming up the sloped lawn to the house. She watches him, unmoved, and tries to remember precisely when it was that she made up her mind not to love him any more. She has learned that life is a lot easier if you keep your choices simple. Not loving Eric was the best way she knew to protect herself and the girls from him.

The sliding door in the kitchen opens and closes and she hears Eric looking through the kitchen cupboards. "Where are all our glasses disappearing to?" he calls out to her.

"The girls keep dropping them," answers Anne.

"Bloody kids."

From the kitchen, Eric calls, "Why don't you come down? Mother's going to think you don't like her."

"I don't," Anne answers.

He comes in and sits down beside her. "You really embarrassed me down there," he says. "Everybody wants to know why you're so goddamn touchy."

"Tell them I'm having an attack of sanity."

Anne notes that Eric's hands are shaking, which means he's going to ask her about the money again. These days, he shakes whenever failure is imminent. For instance, when he tries to make love to her, he trembles until his teeth chatter.

"Let's go out tonight," Eric says. "Just you and me."

"What for?"

"We never talk like we used to."

"If you want to talk to me, all you have to do is turn off the television during supper."

"The kids would interrupt."

"Look, Eric," warns Anne. "Don't get coy with me. I know what you want. I told you before, I told you a hundred times, I can't give you the money." Eric wants to invest the rest of Anne's inheritance in a tavern that is up for sale in a nearby town. "That money is my nest egg," she says. "Besides, Daddy wouldn't have wanted me to spend it that way."

"When you met me, you didn't give a damn about Daddy."

"I know," says Anne. She looks at Eric's bewildered face and bites her lip, momentarily torn. "Let me think," she says, to appease him temporarily. "Let me think about the money." But thinking about the money is no use, because Anne's inheritance is quickly draining away in payments to her analyst, whom she is seeing on the sly. It is he who told her to smash the drinking glasses, to employ her anger in an empowering way. Better to smash a glass than Eric or herself, he told her.

———

At three o'clock in the afternoon, the sun and the gin drive Mrs. King into the house. She falls onto Desiré's bed and snores. Lance plays Parcheesi with the children in the living room. Reed and Eric have taken the sailboat out on the river. Anne goes outside to weed her rose bed. She hears snatches of dialogue carrying across the water from other cottages. "My God!" a woman's voice exclaims, "—*freezing*!" Standing up to stretch her legs, Anne notices that Eric's sailboat has pulled in at a dock further down the river. She sees Reed leap out, another figure climb in, then Reed push the boat off, hopping in himself. The boat heads out into the wind again, rocking as the sails fill. Anne moves quickly down the lawn to the patio, squats and scans the river with the telescope until she picks up the boat. On the deck with Eric and Reed, she sees the blonde girl, Judith, wearing a bikini. She is sitting in the stern of the boat, beside Eric, who guides her hand on the tiller. Now the boat slips behind an island in the river, disappearing from view. "Damn that Eric!" mutters Anne, jerking the telescope away from her face so that it spins round and round on its pedestal, like a pointer on a board game. "Damn, damn, damn!" She begins to walk away, then turns and kicks the telescope over.

———————

Mrs. King is still sleeping at six o'clock. Anne, now wearing a white sleeveless blouse and a pair of yellow shorts in which she looks hippy and graceless, brings hamburgers, hot dogs and buns out onto the deck and starts the barbecue. She returns to the kitchen and is tearing lettuce into a large wooden bowl when Reed comes in for another beer. "What about my two hundred dollars?" Anne asks him quietly without turning around.

"It's in the bank," Reed says, popping off the bottle cap. "I'll write you a cheque before I leave." They both know that he is lying. Reed reaches for the sliding door.

"Listen," Anne says quickly, her eye dwelling once again on his slender thighs. "Listen, forget the money. It doesn't matter. I was wondering what your plans are for tonight. I mean, I thought we might go for a walk. The woods are lovely now, in the evening. Eric will probably be in his workshop. Your mother can watch the children. We could slip away quietly." She wants to find out, she wants to know, if Reed finds her attractive or if he was kissing her that time just to undermine Eric in some sick way that only a King could understand. And has she—has Anne—been infected with that same sickness? she wonders. Does she want to touch Reed now, to press her body against the length of his in order to punish Eric for flirting with that girl, that babysitter she's pretty sure he once spent three hours making a pass at?

Reed frowns and shakes his head. "Sorry," he says. "I'm going to the dance tonight with Judith."

———————

Jade and Desiré, bathed and in pink nightgowns, are chasing each other on the lawn. Cassandra, the baby, has been put to bed. The river is indigo in the evening light and there are enormous clouds hanging in the sky. Anne carries the salad out onto the deck and sits down at the table, where the others have started eating without her.

"Did anybody check on Mother?" asks Reed.

"Dead to the world," Lance grins, shaking his head fondly.

"It's nice to have her out here helping with things," quips Anne.

"If you were as old as *her*—" says Eric.

"I wonder who'll be at the dance," says Reed, taking some salad.

"Everybody," says Eric gloomily, drumming his fingers on the table.

"I thought about renting a movie," says Anne to Eric. "I could make popcorn. We could have a nice quiet evening together."

"Are you going to the dance?" Eric asks Lance.

"Not me!" chuckles Lance. "I learned a long time ago that girls just get you in trouble."

"The best kind of trouble there is," observes Reed.

"I wonder if they need any help behind the bar," says Eric.

"You promised to give up the club," Anne reminds him. "You said no more hangovers."

"I hear the place is going to hell without me," Eric addresses Reed, looking for sympathy. "I helped build that club with my own hands. I care about it."

But Reed is not listening. "Gotta get going," he says, wiping his mouth with a napkin and standing up. "Gotta shower and shave."

Lance rises too, hiking his pants up over his big belly, and calls down to the girls, "Hey, you two, how about a game of hide-and-seek?"

"Don't anybody rush to help with the dishes," says Anne.

Eric looks at her critically. After the others have gone, he asks, frowning, "Why do you have to be such a bitch?"

"I don't know," she says, smiling glassily. "It seems to be my lot in life, doesn't it?"

At seven thirty, not wanting to wake Mrs. King up, Anne puts Desiré and Jade together in Jade's bed. Lance will sleep tonight on the couch, his long legs hanging over the end, and Reed, if he returns from the dance at all, will sleep on cushions on the living-room floor.

Anne picks up the girls' damp swimsuits from the floor, closes the bedroom door quietly and goes into the bathroom to hang them up on a rod. There, she notices, through the bathroom window, Reed and Eric up on the incline behind the house, under the tall pine trees. Pressing her face to the screen, she tries to hear what they're saying, but they're too far away. Then she sees Eric shove Reed roughly in the shoulder with the heel of his hand and Reed push him back in the chest. Eric takes a swing at Reed's head, but Reed, younger and more fit than Eric, ducks the punch. He straightens up, leering, and his clenched fist shoots out at Eric's face, knocking him backward onto the ground.

"I'm out'a here, man!" Reed shouts with disgust, turning and walking up the needle-covered incline to his Jeep.

"Fuckin' jerk!" Eric calls, still sitting on the ground. Reed stops beside his car, takes out a cigarette and lights it coolly. "Fuckin' asshole!" Eric shouts up the hill. Reed gets into his Jeep, starts the engine and tears up the hill. Eric touches his nose gingerly, brings his hand away and sees blood on his fingers. A minute later, he is in the bathroom, splashing cold water on his face. The blood has run down his arm and is all over the front of his shirt.

"What was that all about?" Anne asks him, pulling a towel off a rack. "Here, let me see your face."

"Never mind," Eric says angrily, pushing her aside, "I'm all right." He removes the shirt, throws it on the floor and goes into the bedroom. Anne picks the shirt up, fills the sink with cold water and puts the shirt in, squeezing the water through it. Then she goes into the bedroom, where she sees that Eric has pulled on his black dress pants and is in front of the mirror, buttoning up the paisley shirt she gave him for his birthday.

"You should lie down until that nose stops bleeding."

"It's fine now. It's nothing."

"Why were you and Reed fighting? I want to know."

"It's got nothing to do with you," he says, picking a comb up from the dresser and running it through his hair. "It's just between the two of us, so lay off."

"You're fighting about that babysitter, that Judith, aren't you?"

"I told you it's none of your business," says Eric, putting his wallet and change in his pockets.

"You're after that poor kid, aren't you? Is she sixteen yet? You could get jailed if you don't keep your cock in your pants."

"You're fuckin' paranoid, you know that?" he shouts at her. Then more calmly, he says, "Look, I go crazy, cooped up here at night. I need to get out. I'm just going over to the club and have a few drinks with the boys. Don't wait up for me."

Anne follows him into the hall. "You promised me you'd start staying in at night. You said you'd start taking an interest in the girls." Without answering, Eric walks through the living room and disappears out the back door. Anne goes back into the bathroom and looks out the window. She sees Eric heading for the car, jingling his keys.

She shouts out the window, "If I end up getting bloody AIDS from you, I'm going to take that gun of yours and blow your fucking pecker off!"

When the car has roared up the hill to the road, Anne closes her eyes, clenches her hands into fists and pounds her knuckles on her head until it's ringing. Weeping, she leans on the windowsill and bites hard on the back of her hand. She tastes blood. Across the hall from the bathroom, the door to Desiré's room suddenly opens and Mrs. King appears, her hair tousled. Anne straightens up quickly, thankful that the bathroom and hallway have grown dim in the softening evening light.

"What's all the shouting? Where is everybody?" yawns Mrs. King, coming forward to turn on the bathroom light and peer into the mirror.

"They've gone to the dance."

"Eric too?"

"Yes."

"Those boys!" cries Mrs. King cheerfully. "They've broken my heart a thousand times. Look at this *hair*!" she says despairingly, pulling at it as though it were alive. She turns and sees Anne's red eyes. "Have you been crying?" she asks, but does not come forward to comfort her. "What's the matter?" she asks in a practical, challenging tone. "Is it Eric? I don't know what I can say. You knew what he was like when you married him, didn't you? A party hound from way back. His father was a boozer, so what can you expect? You can't ask a man to sit home all the time. I tried to make Eric's father do it and look what happened."

In the living room, Anne finds Lance in front of the television.

"Eric went to the dance," she tells him.

"I know," he says. "I figured he would." He picks up the remote control and changes the station.

Anne sits down in a chair in a dark corner of the room, where she has a view of the river. She hears Mrs. King running water in the bathtub. Looking out at the evening, Anne says, "You know the first time Eric and I had sex?"

"No," says Lance absently, absorbed in the television.

"It was in the back of his car on a night like this. We'd met at a party that evening, up here in the country. Eric gave me my first joint. He knew I was a virgin—he could spot one a mile away. He offered to drive me home, but instead we went parking. One thing led to another. The next thing we knew, a police car had pulled up beside us. Eric was dressed and out of the car before I had even reached for my clothes. I couldn't make out what he and the officer were saying, but finally they laughed together. Eric knew every cop in the district, and they knew him, of course, by reputation. Eric opened the car door and leaned in. 'He wants some information,' he said to me, 'and I realized I don't know your name.'"

Anne turns and sees that Lance hasn't heard a word. Finally he senses her looking at him and glances over at her.

"Did you say something?" he asks.

Anne laughs ruefully and gets up. "No, nothing at all," she answers, passing behind him. She slides the screen door open and steps out onto the deck, inhaling the soft night and the weedy smell of the river. In the sky floats a cloud shaped like a white ship, full of innocence and promise. Anne leans with both hands flat on the railing and sighs.

"You could go out too and tie one on," Lance calls encouragingly from the living room.

"I'm too old for that. I'm over the hill."

"No you're not, you're still beautiful," says Lance, and raises the volume on the TV.

For Anne, there is a sadness in the evening, in the slow, glassy movement of the river, the deserted deck with towels drying on the empty chairs, the hollow drilling of a woodpecker in a tree, the memory of cool-cheeked girls on summer nights like this, when white ships sail in the sky.


## II


"What were you doing back there?" Anne asks Eric. "I told you I don't like you creeping around the bedrooms. It makes me nervous. I want you to stay in the living room when you're here, or outside, where I can keep an eye on you." She's in the kitchen, cutting the string off the bakery box containing the cake for Jade's sixteenth birthday. Anne is wearing her hair in a short, modern cut. She's lost some weight in the past few years, and now she has a leanness of neck and jaw that is not altogether attractive. It makes her look older and tougher, like a piece of driftwood stripped of its bark.

"I wasn't doing anything," says Eric sheepishly. His hairline has receded noticeably and there is a look of defeat and caution about him and also a certain quality of injury in his face that Anne believes he cultivates to prey on her conscience. "I just like to look around when I come up," he tells her innocently. "You know. Renew old acquaintances. Sometimes when I'm lying in my apartment at night I try to remember how the different rooms in the house look, where the furniture is placed exactly and what colour the walls are and the curtains."

Lifting the cake out of the box, Anne pauses to look at him. "You're getting weird," she says, unsympathetic, and licks some icing off her thumb.

"You don't know how lonely it is living by yourself."

"I would have thought you'd be laying everything in sight, now that you're free."

"You're the only woman I want," says Eric.

"Fine time to decide that," says Anne. She has noted Eric's dress pants and his flowered Italian shirt, which she knows he's put on in an attempt to make himself attractive to her. She should tell him it's no use. Anne now believes that there is a brief moment in life when a woman is young and generous with herself and susceptible to love. If she throws that moment away on a man like Eric, she doesn't get any more chances. She had had hopes of meeting someone else after she threw Eric out two years ago. She had started to take better care of herself, but there did not seem to be any good prospects out there. She is not even sure why she'd want to meet another man. She does not think she believes in love any more.

In a few weeks, Anne and Eric's divorce will be final. Eight years ago, Anne reluctantly handed over what was left of her inheritance to Eric to buy the tavern he wanted. The business limped along for six months, then folded. That was when Anne decided to give up her psychiatrist and go out and get a job. Eventually, she set up a small business of her own, handling office moves, arranging for vans, packing up equipment, moving furniture from old offices to new ones. She has a crew of ten men working for her. Eric, who is on unemployment insurance because of civil service cutbacks, has asked if she'll give him a job and she has refused. She is looking forward to signing the divorce papers, to putting the marriage behind her, but Eric is still hoping for a reconciliation.

"I was looking at the outbuildings earlier," Eric says. "I noticed that the door of the shed is hanging on one hinge and there are a dozen or so loose shingles on the workshop roof. I put a lot of work into those buildings. I hate to see them going to hell."

"If I had the money, I'd get them fixed," says Anne, rummaging in a drawer. "I was sure I had some birthday candles somewhere."

"Why pay someone to do it when I could come up anytime—"

"The judge *said*," Anne cuts in impatiently, slapping her hand down flat on the counter while glaring at Eric, "six months before you see the girls. I think that's a good stretch for you to get your act together. Also, it gives them time to get over your little drama. I was crazy to let you come up here today, but you got Jade so worked up I had no choice. You shouldn't have phoned her. That was against the rules too. Don't pretend you don't know it. My lawyer would have my head if he knew you were here. I hope you're going to behave yourself today."

"I promise I'll be a good boy," says Eric somewhat mockingly and Anne gives him a stony look.

"What's Lance doing here, anyway?" Anne asks. "And your mother? I don't remember inviting them. I'm not sure there's enough cake now."

"They wanted to see Jade. They wanted to see *you*."

"Sure they did."

"Mom was driving downtown the other day and she saw you on the street dressed in one of your business suits, carrying your briefcase and all. She was impressed as hell."

"She's sure got old and sour," observes Anne. This is the first she's seen of Mrs. King in a year. The last time was when Eric was admitted to the hospital after swallowing a bottle of sleeping pills.

"It wasn't a genuine suicide attempt," Anne, who'd responded reluctantly to a phone call, told Mrs. King at the hospital. They were standing beside Eric's bed in the psychiatric ward. He was sleeping, under sedation. Anne looked down at him, unmoved. "He's just trying to get attention," she told Mrs. King. "He's trying to get back at me. If he'd really been serious about killing himself, he would have blown his brains out. It's not as if he didn't have enough guns handy to do it with."

"He was the best father he knew how to be," said Mrs. King. "He had nobody to teach him."

"He never learned how to love," Anne told her. "He may not have had a decent father but you could have taught him that much, at least. But I guess you have to know how to love before you can teach someone how."

Then Mrs. King had started to weep. "I'll never forgive you for saying such a thing," she told Anne.

"I don't want your forgiveness," Anne told her. "I got your son and that was more than I could stand."

A few months ago, Eric turned up unexpectedly at the house one Sunday afternoon, saying he wanted to talk to Anne and the girls. He got them to sit in a row on the couch and he sat down in an armchair opposite them and pulled a revolver out of his pocket. He held it to his temple and said that if any of them moved or spoke, he'd blow his head off. Then he told them the whole story of his pathetic life, about how his father had pickled his liver and beat Mrs. King and the boys before finally kicking the can when Eric was only ten. About what a failure he was at school. About a series of close scrapes with the law during his teen years. About hating his job until he found unemployment was even worse than working. About living alone in a sterile apartment and missing them all, especially the girls, and still loving Anne with all his heart and feeling now like he wasn't worth two cents, and the only thing that kept him every day from jumping off his apartment balcony was hope. Hope that Anne would take him back. It took an hour to get all this out, during which time the girls, frozen in their seats, wept and trembled and came close to throwing up.

Anne heard him out and then said, "Well, I've got better things to do than sit around here listening to this garbage. I've got vacuuming, and if you want to pull the trigger, be my guest, it's your stupid life." She got up, went down the back hall and pulled the vacuum out of a closet. She plugged it into a wall socket in the hall and roared into her bedroom with it. There, she picked up the phone and dialled 911. "There's a madman loose in my house with a gun," she said into the receiver. The police arrived within minutes and took Eric away in handcuffs.

Now Eric is seeing a psychiatrist, on a court order. Before the separation, Anne had asked him to see an analyst, but he'd just laughed at her. "Shrinks are for nuts," he'd said. Now his shrink is all he can talk about. "I'm sick," he tells people unabashedly, slightly boastful, scratching the back of his head. My shrink says this and my shrink says that. "My shrink wants me to take these pills, for a while anyway." And, "My shrink says it all goes back to my father."

"Don't think having a lousy father absolves you of responsibility," Anne told him.

---

"If there isn't enough cake, I don't have to have any," says Eric, full of self-sacrifice. He has insisted on carrying the paper plates, napkins and plastic forks down to the patio, though Anne says to him, "Why lift a finger now when you never did before?" Anne follows him down to the river, bearing the cake, flaming with candles.

The afternoon is hot and humid. There is a pearly light over the sluggish water that distorts vision, giving the illusion that the river is wide, wider than it actually is, that they are standing in a dream, with the real world pushed back to a far, far shore. This is the kind of perfect, windless day that makes the sky seem deeper, the clouds more baroque, the daylight hours longer than anywhere else in the world. Anne wishes the river weren't such a picture because she knows it will fill Eric with a maudlin nostalgia.

Now she is bent over a low table, serving up the cake.

"Oh, Mom," says Jade, mildly reproachful, teasing, "you're going to let Dad have a piece of *cake*, aren't you?" A lifetime up here in the country, beside the river, has turned her into a bronzed, athletic girl, with a healthy glow. Her crimped, strawberry-blonde hair measures to her elbow, and she has a fine, long nose and white, white teeth. Eric has told Anne that every time he sees Jade, he's shocked by her beauty.

"She hasn't made any mistakes with her life yet," Anne said. "That's why she's still beautiful."

Desiré and Cassandra, who have been swimming with Lance, come out of the river to get a piece of cake. They are fourteen and twelve, both of them with dark curls. Eric, now that he's not living with them any more, now that, as he says, he misses them like crazy, seems to be able to remember their names.

Jade, sitting on one of the patio chairs, is opening Eric's gift. He's bought her a compact disc player.

"How much did *that* cost?" asks Anne, who has been paying matrimonial support to Eric ever since they separated.

"It was on sale," says Eric evasively.

"Aw, Dad, don't tell me *that*," says Jade. "It spoils it."

"*You're* spoiled," says Eric, pleased with himself, as though he can take sole credit for it.

"It seems to me," says Anne to Eric, "you could be less frivolous with my money."

"These days, in a divorce," says Mrs. King regretfully from a chair in a corner of the patio, "women have all the power." Mrs. King suffered a mild stroke soon after Eric's suicide attempt. Although it didn't impair her speech or mobility, she has a blanched look now, as though she has seen her own ghost. She's not exactly fragile yet, but she seems to have lost physical mass, and moves carefully these days, gripping doorknobs and the arms of chairs whenever she can, as though her bones have become hollow and weightless and she fears she might float weightlessly up into the sky if she doesn't hold herself down.

Lance, water streaming from his swimsuit onto the patio, eats a piece of cake right out of his hand. He hasn't gotten thinner with time. His stomach is like a great, white balloon in danger of bursting. He is always boasting that he hasn't seen his toes in years. "Hey, you guys," he reproaches Eric and Anne gently, grinning, icing on his face, "I thought this was supposed to be a party."

"*Yeah*, Mom," says Jade, scowling at Anne.

Eric's attention is caught by a movement up on the hill. "Well, lookee who's here," he says without pleasure. They turn to see Reed round the corner of the house. For the past few years he's been working in the oil fields, at isolated camps in northern Alberta. The money is good in that business and his only complaint is that there are no women to be had. He comes back home once or twice a year, but, as far as they know, keeps pretty much to himself. Now he lopes down the hill toward them, long-legged, loose-jointed, wearing black skin-hugging jeans, a black shirt, cowboy boots and a Stetson.

"Looks like Palladin," says Lance.

"What's *he* doing here?" asks Eric, narrowing his eyes at Anne. "Who invited *him*?"

"If the rest of you can come up here and park yourselves, why shouldn't *he*?" says Anne with a shrug.

"Who's Palladin?" asks Cassandra.

---

At five o'clock, Anne still hasn't been able to get rid of Eric and Mrs. King. Jade, dressed to go out, comes into the kitchen, where Anne is wiping the counter.

"Why don't you let Daddy stay for supper?" she asks. "He came all this way. The least you could do is feed him. All you've given him since he got here is one little piece of cake. He's been really sweet today, don't you think?"

Jade and Anne do not see eye to eye on Eric. "I can't believe," says Anne, "that you can be so easily sucked in by him. Don't you remember how he used to talk to you? He used to treat you like *shit*."

"Well," says Jade smugly, "I know how to forgive."

"You can afford to forgive. You've got the rest of your life ahead of you. But be careful. People don't change. They pretend to change, but in the long run they don't. They just stay their same old rotten selves."

Jade looks at her pityingly. "You're getting really cynical, you know that?" she says unhappily. "In fact, you've gotten to be a real *bitch*."

"Have I?" says Anne lightly, with a cold smile. "Well, this bitch is clothing and feeding you."

Jade picks up her purse angrily and strides out the front door.

"Happy birthday!" Anne calls after her, her voice full of irony.

A few minutes later, Eric comes in, wearing his bathing suit and drying the back of his neck with a towel. "Nice to get in the river after so long," he says, but Anne ignores the remark. She has become adept at stepping around Eric's hints that he'd like to move back in with her. Mrs. King comes into the kitchen, too, and stands by the door. Ever since Anne's remark at the hospital, there has been a stone wall between them. Eric pulls a shirt on over his head. "Where'd Jade go? I saw somebody come and pick her up in a car."

"She's gone out with her friends to celebrate."

"Where to?"

"She never tells me," says Anne. "They'll probably end up at the club later on."

"That's no place for her," says Eric.

"I've talked to her about birth control."

"Birth control!" says Eric. "Christ! She's only sixteen!"

Anne smiles at him sweetly. "The shoe's on the other foot now, and it pinches, is that it?"

Eric suggests that he take Cassandra and Desiré out for a ride in the sailboat, but Anne tells him they've walked into the nearby town with Lance to see an early movie. Lance will stay overnight and catch a ride home into the city with Reed.

"Reed?" says Eric.

"Yes," says Anne. "He's offered to stay over to work on those shed repairs you mentioned."

Eric snorts, incredulous. "That's a good joke," he says sarcastically. "He doesn't know the right end of a hammer."

"I'm sure he'll manage," says Anne. "I think it's time you left, Eric. You wouldn't want to overstay your welcome, would you?" she adds with sweet sarcasm.

In the bathroom, Eric changes from his bathing suit to his slacks and comes out to the kitchen again, his rolled-up towel under his arm. Passing Anne, who is picking over some fruit in a big wooden bowl, he says, "Your hospitality has been overwhelming," and goes out the sliding-glass door.

Mrs. King picks up her purse. Anne notices how stooped she's become and how her dark lipstick bleeds like paint into the puckers around her mouth. Before turning to go out, Mrs. King looks at Anne sternly. "You can get the law to restrict Eric from coming here," she said, "but you can't keep his heart away from this place."

Anne stands there pressing the navel of a cantaloup experimentally with her thumbnail. She raises her eyebrows and says pleasantly, "That's odd. When he lived here with me, his heart always seemed to be somewhere else. All he wanted to do was get out. Why would that be? Maybe it was the recollection of you with a two-by-four in your hand."

Mrs. King ignores the remark, as though the stroke damaged her hearing. "This house will always belong to the Kings, no matter who holds the mortgage," she says. "It's ours and so is the river."

Just then they hear shouting from outside. Anne drops the cantaloup on the counter and rushes out the door. Mrs. King follows slowly. Up on the hill behind the house, under the inky pines, Reed is sprawled backward across the hood of his car. Eric is standing back with a look of satisfaction, watching Reed cautiously and rubbing his knuckles.

Anne looks at them, her hands on her hips. "What the hell's going on?" she demands. "Who started it this time? I suppose it was you, Eric." Eric does not look at her, but shoves his hands in his pockets. Reed is nursing a cut in a corner of his mouth.

"I must have been out of my mind to let you come up here," says Anne to Eric. "It wasn't for me. It was for you and the girls, and this is the thanks I get for putting up with you all day. You can't get along with anybody, can you, even your own brother? You'll never grow up."

"I saw Reed putting one of my best wrenches in the trunk of his car," Eric says angrily. "He's got no business taking that."

Reed stands up and presses the back of his hand to his mouth.

"Those tools are only half yours," Anne reminds Eric, "and you've got no use for them in an apartment anyway. Now, I want you to clear out of here, or I'll call the cops."

Eric stands there for a moment, clenching his fists, evidently considering his options. At last he says, "Okay, fine. I'll go peacefully. But that doesn't mean I won't be back."

"Oh, you scare me to death," says Anne, mocking him.

"Come on, Mom," says Eric bitterly, getting behind the wheel.

Mrs. King moves slowly to the car and opens her door. She climbs in awkwardly as though she's forgotten what a car is, her legs stiff, her feet clumsy in her thick-heeled shoes, both hands braced on the door frame, her square purse banging against her hip. The car drives off up the hill to the highway, spitting gravel out from under its tires.

Anne leads Reed into the kitchen, where she examines his split mouth.

"Your husband is an asshole," Reed tells her, wincing as she applies ice to his mouth.

"Well, in three weeks he won't be my husband any more, but he'll still be your brother," says Anne, and Reed snorts with bitter amusement.

"Why'd you take the wrench?" she asks.

"I got something I can use it on. D'you mind?"

"No," she says quickly.

"I didn't think you would," he says with a knowing smirk. He takes her hand away from his face, seizes her by the wrist and pulls her roughly toward him. He bends to kiss her and she is lifted back to the summer of the white ship. Now she feels Reed's strong fingers pulling the tails of her blouse out of her shorts, his rough oilman's hands riding up her stomach, pushing back her bra. He kneads her breasts rhythmically, with bruising strength, watching her face. She winces, aroused but torn. Soon they will lie down together, Reed will slide into her, greedy, fugitive, brutal, drive himself deep within her, stirring up old wounds, old desires. Anne wants him. She wants him, and yet. And yet, some part of her is saddened, humiliated by her need to be entered, replenished, completed by this blood brother of her ex-husband, this second son of a woman she hates. For doesn't this make her, when all is said and done, no better than they? All these years when she thought she was so much above Eric's family, so separate from their violence, their disloyal ways, she is still turning to them for sustenance, for approbation.

"Tell you what," Reed says. "Why don't you go and fix yourself up while I smoke a joint? Jesus, I've been waiting for a high all afternoon."

Anne goes into the bathroom to freshen up, then crosses the hall to her bedroom, where she pulls out a drawer, looking for something enticing to wear. She pauses for a moment, stepping to the window to look out. It is nearly eight o'clock and dusk is falling, the grey light flattening the shapes of everything. The river has turned silver in the soft night. Anne watches its steady, drugged current, feels herself pulled down by it. For a moment, she sees herself—a young, rebellious woman many years ago—standing on the shore of the river, flinging her wallet, identification and all, out across the gleaming surface. What I really wanted to do that day, she now realizes, was to throw myself into the river, to free myself of Eric and his family forever, to sink gently beneath the watery surface, sending out a delicate pattern of ripples.

The smell of Reed's joint drifts down the hall to her.

I must go and tell Reed I want him to leave, thinks Anne. But she does not move. She stands at the window biting her nails. I must go and tell him that.

# THE SUM OF ITS PARTS

TARA SAID, "That Irmgard!"

"That Irmgard!" she said one Saturday afternoon at the kitchen table where she was doing her homework.

Franklin was opposite her, sorting his hockey cards.

"That Irmgard! I just love her!" Tara was in the co-op program at school where they go out half-days into the community and work in some job situation to get an idea of different walks of life. Harlan had got her a placement at his school, with the kindergarten teacher.

I said, "Irmgard, Irmgard." I was washing up the lunch dishes. "When will we stop hearing about Irmgard?"

Tara said, "Irmgard's wonderful. Isn't she, Dad?"

Harlan, reading nearby on the family-room sofa, looked up. "She's a very fine teacher," he said neutrally.

"She knows every one of those kindergarten children inside out," Tara told us. "She listens. She understands. She loves them like a mother. She sees their faults and yet she doesn't criticize. She brings out their strengths instead. They adore her."

I said, "You've turned her into a saint because of her wooden leg. Would you canonize me if I had one?" I heard Harlan sigh from the couch.

"Irmgard is strong and deep and good," Tara said, her voice quivering with admiration.

I said, "And, of course, I'm not."

"Why are you so insecure? Why do you take everything personally?" Tara asked bitterly, her eyes blazing at me. The hatred of teenagers is so pure. Pure as the wind. It takes your breath away. Sometimes Tara looked at me with such loathing that I had to wonder who it was she was seeing.

"Did you hear what she said, Harlan?" I demanded, looking to him for support, always a mistake.

"You do seem to be threatened by other people's strengths," he said with gentle honesty.

"Do you think that, Franklin?" I asked, looking at our son, who gave a little, torn smile. He was an expert at skating around conflict.

"I don't suppose we could go down to the store and buy me some more hockey cards?" he said, his voice like a sparrow's song. He was at that golden age of childhood, which seems to fall between the ages of ten and twelve. Children at that age are blessed in a way that they never will be again in their lives. They are full of optimism and naivety and such deep trust in life that it breaks your heart in a way. He played goalie on a bantam team. It was enough to make him happy. Life could be that simple.

Tara said, "I want to model myself after Irmgard. I've decided I'm going to be a teacher."

I said, "A teacher! You're going to throw yourself away on a pack of brats like your father did?"

"What do *you* think I should be?" asked Tara. "A waitress?"— which of course was a dig at me. Then for an instant she looked so like my mother. It was not just the thick black hair falling against the fine bones of her face, but something more—in her expression I saw my mother the blind missionary, the willing victim, the fortress, the wise, profound and unshakable woman I could never reach or understand—and I felt that already Tara had passed me in life somehow.

Of course, then, Tara decided to pack up her books and march off in a huff to work in her room. Franklin slid away from the table too. He had an instinct for seeking out places of calm, like a river flowing gently to the sea.

After they were gone, Harlan sighed that weary little sigh he'd perfected and looked at me tragically, a thick text balanced on his knee. He always had his nose in some book, being what they call cerebral. When I met him I was working down on Elgin Street in a diner and he used to come across from the old stone teachers' college after classes and sit in one of the window booths in the sun, reading some tome and drinking coffee or enjoying a student's supper of minestrone soup. Beyond the window, the world slid past, unnoticed by him. His long flowing hair and full blond beard lent him a biblical look.

"Here comes the prophet Abraham," I'd say to the girls when we saw him come in, and though I joked, I sensed the strength in him. Sitting there in the sun, he seemed to be the source of the light, its power spread out from him miraculously, and along with it a serenity that must have come from the great weight of knowledge he'd amassed in his young head, leaving him at peace, grounded, like a ship at anchor. This aura flowing out from him filled me with irrational hope. One day I went over and handed him an extra paper serviette.

I said, "You have let soup fall in your beard."

"Thank you," he said, taking the serviette and dabbing at his beard. "I am often absent-minded." He looked up at me, searching my face carefully. "Would you like to go to a movie on your day off?" he asked, though it was obvious he'd never seen me before, notwithstanding that I'd been carrying his coffee to him for months, taking special care not to slop it over the rim and sometimes sliding a digestive cookie onto the saucer too. He'd never noticed I hadn't charged him for the cookies, and for all I knew he didn't even remember eating them. His face told me he was fond of people, even of strangers. His expression was warm and spontaneous and so ready to let me in that for just an instant I feared for him. "You are very observant," he said, and he told me he thought I'd be good for him, I'd keep him connected to "real life."

Soon, Harlan was saying he'd never met a girl like me before. He said he loved my skewed sense of humour and my rebelliousness and my strength and he loved my family, because of course I'd taken him home by this time. He said he especially loved my brother Art and I said, "You've got to be kidding." Then Harlan came out with all this psychological bunk about Art being a free spirit and an original personality and misunderstood by society and *blah-blah-blah*, and I told him, "Harlan, you've got a lot to learn."

When we got married, Harlan taught grade one and for a long time I looked up to him and felt proud and amazed to be his wife. After a while, though, I kept expecting him to grow up and get tired of playing with Plasticine and wooden blocks, but he said there was a lot more to his job than that. He got a reputation all over the school board as a progressive teacher, an advocate of what they now call child-centred learning. He moved the desks out of his classroom and put a sofa and an Indian rug in their place to make the children think that learning was not a task but a natural and easy part of life. He got rid of tests and marks and report cards. He was all in favour of self-esteem and emotional growth. Once there was a big article on him in the paper that I cut out and thought about having framed. People began to say to him: Why don't you move on? Why don't you go for principal? Why don't you develop curricula, spread your message from the top down? But he said no, he liked it at the grass roots, he didn't want to lose touch with "The Children." I told him, "You could make more money in administration, you could *be* somebody," but he just gave me that pitying smile I was becoming accustomed to. I told him he wasn't a real man—because you don't see grown men, do you, teaching little kids, it's unnatural?

So on Saturday afternoon, after Tara cleared off to her room, Harlan came to me in the kitchen, walking softly in his bare feet like a Buddhist monk, and laid a heavy book down beside me on the counter.

"What's this?" I said.

"It's all about adolescents and how to deal with them," he said in his best professional voice. "I think you should read it." Beneath the harsh kitchen lights, his head gleamed, for by this time he had grown quite bald. You do often seem to see this in highly intellectual men, these scalps as smooth as an egg, as though the power of their thinking has forced all the hair out.

I said, "I don't need any books on psychology. I know when I'm being talked back to by a teenager." I took the book and dropped it in the dishwater even though it was an old weathered hardcover and probably from the library. Harlan snatched it out before it sank completely and quietly stood it up in the dish drainer, patiently fanning out the pages to dry. He closed his eyes like a priest about to administer a prayer and pinched the bridge of his nose contemplatively with his finger and thumb.

"I'm going out for a walk," he said with great control.

I said, "Where do you go on these walks? You disappear for hours."

"They help me to think."

"Maybe you think too *much*."

The house was very quiet after he left. I went to Franklin, who'd turned on a hockey game on television. He had Harlan's fair colouring, the same translucent skin, the blond eyelashes, the ivory hair, the pale, graceful, feminine hands. He was pure and essential, like sand or a field of wheat.

I said, "Come for a drive with me. We could go and see Grandma and Grandpa."

"Will Art be there?"

"Hopefully not."

"I wouldn't want to go if Art wasn't there."

"What is so wonderful about Art, I'd like to know?"

"I better stay here, Mom," he said from that cool, peaceful centre of his. Sometimes he had a soft way of talking that made him sound like a miniature Harlan. "I need to watch this game."

---

When I reached my parents' apartment I apprehended them in the front hall, on their way out. My mother had put on her ultrasuede coat, which she wears only for special occasions. Each time I saw her now, I had to look twice, because retirement had entirely transformed her. She'd become elegant, happy, young—all the things I'd wanted her to be when I was growing up. Throughout her life she'd worked on the counter of a small dry cleaner, taking in the customers' garments, or matching up their tickets to the dry cleaning that whizzed by on one of those electronic revolving racks, and in between that, working on a sewing machine in a corner doing small repairs, mending seams and replacing zippers. I remember her being tired all the time and wearing faded cotton housedresses and running shoes to work and not taking care of her looks.

But now that she was retired I hardly recognized her. She was unexpectedly attractive, modern and smoothly groomed, with her hair cut straight across at her eyebrows and in a thick wedge to her shoulders, like an Egyptian empress. She'd become what people like to call "a handsome woman." She had height on her side and she carried herself well, with such dignity and poise that people often remarked on it. "It's Art," she'd tell them then. "It's Art who's given me this grace," and I'd say, "It's Art who's turned you grey!"

When they saw me at the apartment door my parents looked guilty, like two kids playing hookey from school. My father stepped behind my mother a little, cowering. It was sometimes a shock to see him alongside her because he was so diminutive, with a bald, grapefruit-sized head, a distracted, nervous and unkempt man meant to be a child all his life.

Behind my parents, sunshine streamed into the living room through a bank of windows. They lived with Art in this new subsidized seniors' building, high up, on the seventeenth floor, a very contemporary apartment full of light, with champagne broadloom, curved white walls, a modern kitchen. Everywhere windows looked out at sky, a wide swath of grassy park, deciduous forest, civilized traffic passing far below on a boulevard curving beside the black river. From this height, the world looked beautiful, kind, good, which suited my parents and Art fine because whenever real life had turned ugly, they'd invented a reality of their own.

I thought it was interesting that they'd waited until I left home before they managed to secure a nice place to live, when all through my childhood they were waking Art and me up in the middle of the night to escape the landlord and move under cover of darkness to yet another small, dim apartment where they'd get into arrears again with the rent because my father went through life smiling idiotically to himself and having nervous breakdowns, though they did not call them that back then.

"Where are you going?" I asked them.

"Oh, just out for a drive," they said cautiously, their eyes sliding away. I knew that look.

I said, "You're going down to the police station, aren't you?" They stared down at the carpet, uncomfortable, sheepish. "Art's been picked up again, hasn't he?" I said. "More shoplifting."

"Oh, it was harmless," my father said quickly, stepping out now where I could see him, enthusiastic as a door-to-door salesman, his face glowing. "It was just a little wallet. Practically of no value. Such a fuss. Those places, Eaton's and those big department stores, they have huge inventories. A wallet here, a lighter there. What is that to them? They're hardly missed. Why do they pick on poor Art?"

"He's just bored with life," said my mother. "He doesn't mean any harm. It's his only bad habit. Everyone's entitled to a few faults. We can't expect him to be perfect."

"The boy just wants to experiment."

I said, "He stopped being a boy a long time ago. Didn't he turn thirty-two last month?"

My father said, "He has a creative streak. He likes to try out different strategies. The methods he comes up with are ingenious."

I said, "That must be why he keeps getting caught."

"He's always operated on a small scale. He's never exceeded theft under two hundred. Why don't they go after the big guys?"

"You should leave him in the tank until he learns a lesson," I told them.

"Oh, that wouldn't be fair."

"We'd miss him."

"Art is used to his own bed."

"I'm going with you," I said. "I want to speak to him."

They looked alarmed. "It would be better if you didn't come," they told me. "Art likes to keep a low profile when he's released."

"I'll help you deal with the authorities."

"But we know the ropes. We could bail him out with our eyes closed."

"It's a wonder they haven't locked the two of you up, as accessories."

"How is Harlan?" they asked, hoping to distract me. They always wanted to know about Harlan.

I lost my temper then. "What's Harlan got to do with it?"

"We love him. He's a wonderful son-in-law."

---

We got in the car and drove downtown, my father in the back seat looking very pleased, grinning senselessly out the window. He was a great watcher of police dramas on television and he enjoyed going down to the station because it brought him in contact with the tangible worlds of crime and law enforcement, which he saw as the two great forces in the universe. I sensed his spirits and my mother's lifting as we proceeded downtown. This was a welcome outing for them. Rescuing Art raised them into another plane of experience, gave them a mission, made them part of something bigger than themselves, a larger-than-life plot.

Their happiness reminded me of the time Art was in the pen for accidentally having a knife in his pocket when he held up a gas station cashier. For two whole years they travelled down to Kingston on the train every Monday to visit him. My mother packed a little picnic lunch for them and they rode cheerfully along in a vacation mood, soothed by the measured swaying of the train, drinking hot tea out of a thermos, eating cucumber sandwiches, enjoying the landscape sliding by the windows, so harmless and serene, talking in optimistic tones about their meeting with Art as though they were visiting a son attending college. My mother said these journeys gave definition and meaning to their lives, they marked off the weeks, made the year pass more rhythmically. Visiting Art got them out of the city and into the open countryside, where my father, looking out the window, counted the silos and watched for groundhogs in the ditch.

My father liked the penitentiary. He described for me its setting, on the shores of Lake Ontario with a pretty view of the marina, as though it were a holiday resort. He was fascinated by the barbed wire strung along the thick outer walls, the armed guards stationed in the corner towers as in a medieval castle, the electronic surveillance system, the big iron doors that rose and fell with a great crash, much like he'd seen in films. In the visiting room, he enjoyed talking into the microphone to Art, who sat on the other side of a glass partition, delivering his lines like a movie actor.

At the police station, my father nearly leapt out of the car before I had a chance to stop, he was so excited to get inside. We entered a large empty lobby, where an officer sitting at a counter instantly recognized my parents.

"Go right on in, Mr. and Mrs. Smirlie," he said in a friendly way.

They smiled and waved at him. "Thank you, Roddy," they called. We passed through into a small waiting area where there was a row of hard chairs to sit down on. Soon Art came loping through a door, looking cheerful and relaxed. He had a bushy handlebar moustache and an absurd mane of long seventies hair that made him look like an aging hippie. People noticed him, he stood out, which wasn't smart. You want to blend into the coatracks and the décor if you're fond of shoplifting. But he also had a boyish look— big apple-red cheeks, comical gaps between his teeth, sparkling blue eyes that seemed to endear him to people.

"Mariah, you old bounder!" he boomed when he saw me and he clapped me on the back. Art is very *joie de vivre*. "What are you doing here? You didn't come down just to see little brother, did you? What happened? Did old Harlan finally boot you out?"

"I came to give Mother and Father moral support."

"We told her not to come," my father told Art quickly. "We told her we had our own way of doing things. We have our little traditions to observe."

"So you lifted a wallet," I said to Art.

"It was a beauty, too," he confided in a low tone. "Italian kid leather. Hand stitched. Special foldout panel for credit cards. State of the art in billfolds. It was for Dad's birthday."

"He never forgets my birthday." My father beamed at him.

I said, "I don't either, but I don't steal what I give you."

"We don't like to call it stealing," said my father delicately. "We think of these things as long-term loans."

By the time the release papers had been signed it was five o'clock and dark outside. We went out and got into the car.

"Don't take us home," my father told me. "Just drop us off at Luigi's."

I said, "What for?"

"It's Art's favourite restaurant. We like to take him out somewhere nice after he's been to the station. It cheers him up."

"He doesn't look too depressed to me."

"It's one of our small ceremonies."

"I'll come too, then. I haven't eaten out in a long time."

"But it's only a table for three," said my mother hastily. "They're very crowded on Saturday nights. The early-bird special. They could barely squeeze us in."

"I can't remember the last time you took me to a restaurant."

"You have your family life. We don't like to disturb you."

When I stopped the car in front of Luigi's, Art and my father got out of the back seat. It was snowing softly. Up and down the road the streetlights floated in the sky like a string of pale moons. It was the kind of soft evening that makes you think life could be turned back to a gentler time. My mother was about to get out of the car. I reached over and grasped her arm to hold her back. The soft cuff of her ultrasuede coat brushed my wrist.

I said, "What do I have to do to make you and Dad notice me? Rob a bank?" She looked at me blankly. She was not a person I had ever known, she was a woman who had waited until I left home to acquire an equilibrium, a symmetry. Her stockings, boots, coat were all grey, the same colour as her hair. She'd become a monochromatic, seamless woman. There was no place for me to get in. Art was calling. He held the restaurant door open, waiting for her to come.

"You've always been strong," she said. "You never needed us as much as Art did."

I said, "If he needs you so much more, why is he the happy one?"

"You have everything a person could want," she told me. "A husband. A nice home. Two beautiful children. You just don't try very hard to be happy."

———

Harlan did not come home that night, which had never happened before. I lay awake wondering where he was. About seven in the morning I heard the front door open and the sounds of him moving around in the rooms below. I put on my housecoat and went downstairs.

"That was truly the mother of all walks, that one you took yesterday!" I said. "Where did you go? Around the world?"

"Something like that," said Harlan quietly, and there was a final note in his voice that drew me up short. He was always a serious man but that morning his face was filled with a kind of determined sorrow. Then I noticed he held two suitcases, which he'd carried up from the basement.

I said, "What are you doing?" and I felt within myself a strange and unsettling stillness like when the wind suddenly drops. I noticed I'd stopped breathing.

He said, "You know how Tara says she loves the kindergarten teacher? Well, I love her too. I've loved her for over a year."

"I don't believe you," I said, though of course I did. It is always the most incredible things that are easiest to believe.

"I'm leaving you. I'm moving in with Irmgard. She is the most profound person I have ever met. I couldn't begin to list for you her qualities."

"I'm not interested in hearing a list about Irmgard!" I said. "I've already heard enough about her to last me the rest of my life!"

"Can you keep your voice down? The children are sleeping."

"I know what my children's habits are!"

"Let them rest."

"Why should I? Why not get them up and tell them what you're about to do to our lives?"

"They stand to benefit from my decision. Contact with Irmgard will enrich them. It's already enriched Tara."

I followed him upstairs to our bedroom. "All this time," I said, "you've been talking to me about Irmgard's art projects, Irmgard's nutritious snacks, Irmgard's phonetic methods and it wasn't her study plans you were admiring, you were lusting after her body." I thought about him longing for Irmgard's legs, the wooden one that came off and the good one that would of necessity be strong and straight to compensate for the bad.

Harlan said, "Irmgard understands what I'm trying to do with my life."

He opened the suitcases on the bed, where the mattress still held the warmth of my body, on the very spot where I'd lain all night sleepless and worrying that he'd been struck by a car, when in actual fact he was lying in a kindergarten teacher's arms. He pulled open drawers and closets, pressed into his bags the simple wardrobe required for his journey toward Irmgard.

I said, "Have you forgotten why you married me?"

"I don't remember any intelligent reasons."

"What about my strength? You said you loved my strength."

"I did think that it was strength you had, but now I understand that it was only anger."

The children came out of their rooms and stood in the doorway wearing their pyjamas.

I told them, "Your father is leaving me for that kindergarten teacher. He's breaking up our home."

Franklin said, "Who will drive me to hockey?"

"If Dad's going to live with Irmgard, I'm going with him," Tara said. "I love Irmgard. I want to be with her." And she went to her room to pack. Franklin disappeared too.

In Tara's room, I watched her dump the contents of her drawers out on the bed. "I don't know how you can make this choice," I told her. "I don't know how you can leave your own mother. It was me who made your baby food and changed your diapers and got up with you at night and sat by your bed when you were sick. It was me, not your father, who was too busy wiping the noses of other people's kids."

Tara said, "That was all a long time ago. I can't even remember any of that stuff. You're different now. We don't get along any more. It's time for us to go our separate directions. You'll see that it's better this way."

Then I went into Franklin's room and found him stuffing things into the big duffle bag he takes to hockey practice: his goalie's gloves and mask, a pair of pyjamas, his hockey magazines, a toothbrush, hockey posters from his walls.

I said, "Franklin, you're not leaving too."

He grimaced apologetically. "I have to, Mom."

"Franklin, I can drive you to your hockey practices."

"But you don't understand the game."

"What is there to understand? There's a puck and a net—"

"Mom," he interrupted sadly, "it's a lot more complicated than that."

"Franklin, I need you here. I need your cheerful outlook on life."

He laid a comforting hand on my shoulder. He seemed suddenly very old and wise. "I'll call you, Mom. We can talk on the phone. All the kids do that. Nobody has married parents any more."

———————

The next day I went out in the morning and walked along the canal, where skaters were stroking smoothly by, oblivious to my grief, selfishly happy. I came to the river and followed that along too, into a neighbourhood of quiet streets and turn-of-the-century clapboard houses with restored gingerbread trim and weathervanes and picket fences. Soon I came to Harlan's school, an ancient brick building with an old-fashioned bell on top. I went inside.

It was a school very much like the one I attended as a child, in a continuous but comfortable state of historic decay, built on a spacious nineteenth-century scale, when the world was evidently a larger place. Milk-glass lights hung by long chains from high, leafy plaster ceilings, the wide staircases were lit by big, ill-fitting windows, above the tall narrow classroom doors, open transoms delivered to me the voices of teachers, voices of children. Somewhere in the building a piano accompanied the singing of a choir. There is always a feeling, in these large, old, overheated schools of dignity, asylum, continuity. And maybe this is what bothered me that day more than anything else, that idea of *continuity*. It crushed me, the sense of something solid and important and timeless going on here, for Harlan, for Irmgard, and me on the outside, not a part of it.

I moved quickly along the hall. A janitor passed by with his mop, but did not ask me what my business was there. Teachers' nameplates fixed to every door helped me find Irmgard's classroom easily enough, in a corner on the first floor. I listened for a moment, heard soft movements, small voices on the other side of the door. The piano music on the second floor ceased. The choir voices faded. Far away a gym teacher's whistle blew. A telephone rang in the nearby office. Somewhere a door opened and closed with a bang, ringing up and down the empty halls. I looked down at my hand, trembling on the doorknob, one part of me astonished to see it there, to find myself standing at all in these foreign, echoing halls, and another part feeling that I'd been on a journey to this destination all my life.

I opened Irmgard's door, threw it open actually. The knob struck the wall, sending down a shower of plaster. There before me was Irmgard leaning over a large low table, administering one of her famous snacks, pouring juice into small paper cups. At similar tables all around, her little charges were reaching for rice cakes, almonds, raisins heaped in bowls. Irmgard looked up and seemed to know me instantly. All the little golden heads turned my way, their faces smooth with surprise. A glorious light flooded the room. Around the walls, finger paintings showed me impossible suns, gay bobbing sailboats, apple trees sagging with fruit, stick figures running, skipping, swinging. The room fell silent.

"Do you know what you've done?" I shouted at Irmgard. "Do you have any idea of the wreckage? You have trapped my husband. You have brainwashed my daughter into loving you. Even my lovely son has defected and joined the great crowd of your admirers. Do you think you have a licence to go around casually destroying things that are whole and beautiful and meant to stay that way?"

Irmgard put down the juice pitcher and took a step, not back, but forward, rocking on the bad hip, her body lurching a little. The great shoe on the end of her wooden leg came down, cumbersome and heavy as a flatiron on the linoleum floor. On that side of her body, her shoulder, her hip drooped noticeably. She looked at me, unblinking, as one might brace themself for the approach of a powerful wind. Perhaps once you've lost a limb, you are able to face anything.

I heard my own hysterical voice flooding out into the hall behind me and I didn't care. For the first time in my life I understood something about Art, his desire to break the rules, to crack things open, to defy, to set himself free. I wanted to blow the whole school wide open, destroy Irmgard and Harlan if I could. Out in the hallway, doors were opening, other teachers wondering what the ruckus was. All around the classroom, at the happy little tables, Irmgard's pupils looked at me, their lower lips quivering, their faces splitting open like young fruit. Some of them began to cry, raisins pinched like insects between their soft fingers. Some spilled their apple juice. Others rose from their chairs and ran to Irmgard, who held out her arms and gathered them in like a shepherdess protecting her flock.

I said, "Do you know how much power I have over you now? I could make this affair public. I could take it to the school board. Have you hauled up for breach of ethics. Immoral conduct. You're not fit to be around young children!" But even as I said this, I saw the innocent children clustered around her seeking shelter from my storm and I knew that all need, all good, would flow forever toward

Irmgard. Out in the hall, footsteps approached, coming at a run. A man in a suit appeared.

He said, "Madam, I don't know what you think you're doing, I don't know who you are—"

I said, "I am Mrs. Harlan Nash who are you?"

"I'm the principal and I'm afraid I must ask you to leave the school at once."

"You can ask till you're blue in the face, but I won't go." I stepped out into the hallway. "Harlan!" I shouted at the top of my lungs, my voice echoing as in a barn. "Harlan, come out and show your face if you've got the nerve!"

The principal ran back to the office. I heard him speaking excitedly to the secretary. When he returned, he said, "I have summoned the police."

Then at the end of the hall, the firedoors at the bottom of a wide staircase swung open and Harlan appeared. He stepped lightly toward us, so at home in that place of learning, with its drafty corridors and rattling windows and high, steadfast ceilings. He came along, dressed in a soft red sweater vest and loose flannel pants, his beard fanning out on his chest like a broom, looking not much older, really, than the student who'd walked into that diner so many years before. There are people who seem to pass through life unscathed, time leaves them alone, maybe because they are floating along on a higher plain, and Harlan was one of those.

And I thought: All these years I haven't taken much notice of what he valued or stood for, but, oh, Lord, now didn't I want to understand so much my insides ached from it? I wished I'd been kinder to this man who had once found it so easy to love me. I wished I'd paid more attention to his qualities instead of mocking him long ago to my friends behind the diner counter.

Just as Harlan reached us, so did the policeman, who had entered the school through the front door and come along the hall with his badge flashing under the milky lights. Harlan didn't even look in my direction. He spoke to the policeman, and I can tell you what he said shocked me so much that I wasn't able to utter another word.

He said, "Could you get her out of here, Officer? She needs psychiatric help. I'm her husband. I should know. I've had to live with her insanity all my life but now I'm finished. I will assist the kindergarten teacher in laying charges. The school board will want her confined as well. We have to keep these dangerous people away from defenceless children. Please take her away."

I went out quietly then with the policeman and got into the patrol car. We hadn't driven more than half a block before I saw Tara coming along the snowy sidewalk, arriving at the school for her coop afternoon. The wind lifted her raven hair from her face and she looked so beautiful and so full of that fresh and youthful despair one sees on teenagers zealous to find their place in this world. I had forgotten that innocence is lost so young. She was sixteen and adrift and now Irmgard was going to be her anchor, when I, her mother, had been near at hand, wanting all the time to reach out and steady her if she would let me. But we don't look, do we, at the help that lives right around us?

I believed the policeman was going to take me down to the station and I thought, Oh, wouldn't Art love to see that? Wouldn't he welcome the opportunity to come down and rescue big sister who has been preaching all these years about his criminality? But a few blocks down the street the policeman made a turn and stopped the car at the edge of a park.

He said, "There's a bench over there. Let's go and look at the river." He was in his late fifties, a hefty but fit, rather attractive greying man with a moustache and a sensitive face. We went and sat on the bench.

He said, "It's been a mild winter. We can at least be grateful for that. The river won't have to be blasted this year. It'll break up on its own. See where the ice is turning blue? That's the first sign of melt."

I didn't know what he was talking about. I was going to say, I don't want to hear about the damned river and how would you know, anyway, and what makes you so sure of everything? but I held my tongue. The river flowed from here to the falls only a few blocks away and I thought, I suppose I could go along there and throw myself over the cataract.

The policeman said, "My wife left me a few years back. She was angry because I never got a promotion. I didn't want one. I was happy on the beat. I liked the contact with people. After she left I spent a lot of time wondering what I could have done differently to make things turn out. I suppose that's natural, but it's a waste of time. The first thing you've got to do is stop blaming yourself."

He said, "That wasn't kind, what your husband said in there about you."

"No, it wasn't."

"He didn't mean it. You find out later they don't mean it. They do want to leave you but the words they use are stronger than what they intend. Time is a great healer. You watch, a year from now, two years, you and your husband will be friends."

"I can't imagine that. I am not a person who forgives."

He said, "I thought that might be the case. I thought by the look on your face."

That made me angry, as my life and the way I looked were none of his business. I said, "Is this what they pay you for, to sit on your behind on a park bench in the middle of the afternoon?"

He cleared his throat then and got up rather awkwardly, his thick shadow falling across my body. "I guess not," he said. He looked at me curiously. "I've been thinking all this time that you look familiar," he said. "Are you any relation to someone named Art Smirlie? You look just like him."

I said, very hostile, "He's my brother and I don't look like him at all."

He said, "Maybe I'm wrong. But I thought there was a resemblance."

After he'd gone away, I sat a while longer on the park bench. I thought about Tara walking along the street, looking so pure and untouchable. I thought back to the day Franklin was born and Tara came to visit me in the hospital. Until then she'd been the apple of my eye. I was holding Franklin in my arms when Tara came into the hospital room and I remember feeling like a big axe had descended and chopped my love for her in half so there'd be some available for Franklin, and nothing was ever the same again between me and Tara. I wondered if my mother felt the same thing about me when Art was born.

Thinking back to before Franklin came along, to when Tara was the only one, it was hard for me to grasp how a person could ever have been so wrapped up in a child as I was, so that I seemed to breathe with the same lungs as she did and think the same thoughts and have the same heart pushing the blood through both our bodies, like Siamese twins. I remembered sitting on the carpet with Tara in our first house, when she was eight months old, so small and light to carry, her resting on my knee and the sun shining through the window on us and me turning the pages of one of those board books showing her bright pictures of trains and clowns, and knowing that I was everything to her. How could something like that change so much? You wish you could go back and start all over.

I thought about Tara and Franklin living with Irmgard, becoming her children, and Harlan forming a fourth party, all of them drawing strength from her wooden leg. It wasn't fair. I pictured Harlan at night, tenderly, reverently unstrapping the leg, light and hollow as a baseball bat, storing it—where? On the bureau? Under the bed? In a closet? I saw him lying down like a healer beside Irmgard, pressing his body up against her asymmetry. And I wished I had a defect that could be so easily removed and hidden from sight.

I did not know what I'd done with my life since I met Harlan in that diner when I was only twenty. While Harlan was growing as a teacher and building a professional reputation for himself and developing an intellectual vocabulary, and while my own children were learning and turning into people I didn't understand—Tara into a young woman I'd somehow lost track of and Franklin into this wise, centred child—what was I doing all that time? I was brooding about Art, wasn't I?

All my married life I'd never questioned Harlan's reasons for picking me for a wife, even in my own mind, I was afraid to question them. I never thought about his reasons and maybe if I had I'd have tried to change myself a little into more the person he thought he'd married or the person he believed I could become.

I took the long walk home then, slowly retracing my steps of that morning. I arrived in our neighbourhood just after the schools let out. All the children were returning home between the high, square snowbanks and I thought: Franklin is not going to come walking up this street today.

Already dusk was falling. In the tall, narrow brick houses, lights were coming on. How many people, I asked myself as I passed these glowing windows, how many people in these houses are managing happiness? I wondered what they, my neighbours, would think, when they learned Harlan had left me, just as all along the street other wives and husbands too, depending on the case, had been abandoned. We take a twisted pleasure, don't we, in seeing life repeat certain painful patterns? We are fortified by the sad statistics of the heart.

It was a soft night. Soon, I thought, the canal will melt and then the river will break up, just as the policeman had said. Spring would come.

I went into the house, pulled off my boots, passed through the silent rooms to the kitchen. I turned the light on over the sink. There I found Harlan's psychology book standing in the dish drainer, its pages entirely dry now and beckoning to me. From their soaking, they'd turned all ripply and beautiful, like the petals of a spring daffodil, transformed by my act of madness. I sat down with the book at the kitchen table and read well into the night.

———————

After Harlan left me, Art said, "What is so terrible about that? There are people everywhere who aren't too happy. People being robbed."

I said, "I guess *you* would know about that, wouldn't you?" But then I thought, What *is* so terrible, seeing as Franklin calls me every day and now I've also got Henry?

Because one day the policeman from the park came to my door. At first I didn't recognize him, he was in civilian clothes, a very chic trench coat and brown suede shoes with brass buckles, and I thought, Who is this man with such a marvellous chest and fine head of hair?

That night, Art called me.

"Did a cop come and see you?" he asked.

I said, "Yes, and I'm in love with him." Though why I'd confide anything personal to Art, I don't know.

Art said, "Well, shit," and I knew from his voice that he was pleased.

Henry cultivates bonsai trees. He clips away at them with a pair of small scissors, he seems to be able to spend hours at it.

"I never saw myself doing anything like this," he tells me happily. "I just discovered it by accident."

He lives on the other side of the river and in his backyard he has created a Japanese garden, with sculpted shrubs and imported rocks and a bed of white sand that he grooms in different patterns with a rake.

I said, "It's so tranquil here, Henry. This is like a Peace Garden."

Henry says that some day he's going to take me to Japan.

Henry also says that what made him notice me in the first place was that I live life with passion, something he admires in a woman.

Every weekend I take Franklin over to my parents' apartment to visit. My mother says, "There's something about you, you're calmer now, Mariah. You seem less driven."

Art is like a second or third father to Franklin and I am willing to let him be. Franklin and Henry have made me see Art's redeeming qualities, which I won't go into now, since I'd still have difficulty naming them. It's more the whole picture rather than the separate pieces. What is it they say? *More than the sum of its parts*, which is a phrase I never really understood, but now I think I have an idea.

# G R A S S

MOM said Stirling was like a time bomb that summer, ready to explode, so when he said one day at lunch, "I'm gonna cut grass," she sat down suddenly at the end of the table and let out a big breath.

"You won't get anybody to pay you to do that," Dad told Stirling. There was no money in our neighbourhood. The year was 1950.

"You'd like to think I couldn't get work just because you haven't got any yourself," said Stirling. He had a tongue on him. "I've got fifteen customers already. Not on this street, but nearby." That made Dad sit up.

"And whose lawn mower are you figuring to use?" he asked Stirling.

"Well, I thought I'd use ours," Stirling answered with a smirk.

"You did, did you?" Dad said, raising an eyebrow. Then he told me to get him a piece of paper and a pencil.

"Let me get this straight," said Dad. "All these customers of yours probably have mowers of their own but you've offered to use ours, is that right?"

"That's what I said."

"And who's paying for the gasoline? That coming out of your pocket?"

"That's right."

"Now, look," said Dad, starting to write down figures. I could see he was excited. Any mention of making money got him interested. "How much are you charging people?" he asked Stirling.

"A flat rate for ten weeks, now to Labour Day," said Stirling sounding proud and know-it-all. "Five dollars for a regular yard. Ten if it's a big one."

Dad wrote it down, straight-faced so far. He was comfortable with a pencil in his hand. He loved any kind of figuring.

"How do you know how many times you're going to have to cut the grass? Could be twice a week in August, weather gets hot enough."

"I never thought of that," said Stirling, getting nervous. By this time Mom had got up and started the dishes, but she kept looking at Stirling and Dad over her shoulder, as if she saw what was coming.

"Two times four, that's eight," said Dad. I could tell he was beginning to enjoy himself. To tell you the truth, I was having a pretty good time myself. "Say you cut it eight times in August and four times in July. That's twelve times, plus once in September probably. Five dollars divided by thirteen. That works out to thirty-eight cents a cut. Now, how much is a gallon of gas?" Dad asked gently. He could be patient when he wanted to make a fool out of you. He liked to pull you in, bit by bit, like a fish on a line.

Stirling was squirming in his chair now, watching Dad's pencil fly across the paper. He kept a package of cigarettes tucked inside the sleeve of his T-shirt and he reached for them now, tapping one out onto the table and lighting up. His big ugly hands were trembling. His fingertips were all swollen where he'd bitten his nails back hard and they were yellow with nicotine.

"How many square yards are there in a normal property and how many do you figure you could cut with a gallon of gas? Then there's your labour. What were you figuring on for an hourly wage? How long do you think you'd take to cut a normal-sized property?

What about maintenance? Oil? Spark plugs? Do you have any idea how much they cost? What if the mower breaks down? Not inconceivable if you drive her hard. May run into parts. If you can't fix her right away, you'd have to get hold of a rental. Daily or weekly charge for that."

"Wear and tear on his shoe leather too," I tossed in, and Dad winked at me.

Stirling was red-faced, looking reluctantly across the table, reading the figures upside-down. Finally, Dad threw his pencil down triumphantly on the table and pushed the paper across at Stirling.

"You're practically paying them to let you cut their lawns for them," Dad said severely. "Do you see that? *Course* you didn't have any trouble finding customers. Lotta people recognize a sucker when they see one coming. I don't suppose you could have asked my advice before you set your price. I don't suppose there's anything I could have taught you about profit and loss."

"I'll go back and tell them something different," Stirling said. "Say my price has gone up."

"No, you won't. You've struck a bargain and you'll stick to it. You won't go back on your word."

Then Stirling slammed outside and Mom said to Dad, "Did you have to be so hard on him? At least he's doing something with himself."

I thought what she meant was Stirling would be out of the house now and not banging doors and smashing things around and standing in front of the hall mirror all the time, combing his hair with one knee bent and his pelvis, tipped at an angle, or picking fights with me so that Mom had to keep saying to him, "I don't know what's got into you!"

But Dad took it different and said, "I'm doing something with myself," and Mom answered, caught off guard but ready to fight all the same, "I don't see you looking for work. I don't see you even picking up the newspaper to search the ads."

Then Dad said, "What I'm doing now has a lot longer range possibilities than just finding a job. I got vision but I'm married to a woman who can't see past her nose."

After that Dad went down to the cellar, where he was spending all his time in the cool temperature making diagrams, trying to invent things. Mom finished up the dishes, out of pride. She wasn't going to let it show that Dad had thrown her off. But after she'd dried the last plate, I heard the screen door swing shut and the latch snap to. I went to the kitchen window and saw her going down the street, her body at a slant and her feet like two pistons churning, and if she hadn't been in such a hurry she would have noticed she forgot to take her apron off. She disappeared up the sidewalk that cut through our block, leading to a better part of town where there was a friend of hers from church, a Mrs. Merrifield, whose husband was fully employed.

---

All through July the days were soft, the shadows deep, and the leaves lifted gently in the breeze, sighing. The sweet smell of fresh-mown grass filled the air. Stirling left the house at eight in the morning, when the sun was still low and filtering in yellow shafts through the trees. He disappeared down the street, pushing the mower lightly with one hand, a bag lunch and the gasoline can in the other. The rattle of the mower wheels, rolling along the sidewalk, was carried back to us like small thunder. We didn't see Stirling all day but in the silent afternoons it seemed we could hear the drone of his mower somewhere in the distance, dreamy and far away as church bells.

The first day Stirling went out, Dad got in the car and drove over to where he was working. He came home rubbing the back of his head and smiling to himself. "Whatever else you might say about Stirling, he takes pride in his work," he told Mom. "Doesn't miss a blade of grass. Leaves a fine geometric pattern on the lawn. Trims the edges down close with a clipper. Nice and polite with the customers."

After that, Dad seemed to respect Stirling more and to take him seriously. When Stirling came home at night, Dad would be waiting for him on the porch. "How did it go today, Stirling? How's the mower performing? Any problems getting her started? Don't forget she's got a sensitive choke. Give her too much choke and you'll flood her." Then Stirling would get impatient with all Dad's advice but Dad would pretend not to notice.

Stirling brought home stories about his customers. They were mostly old women, widows or spinsters who spied on him suspiciously from behind their curtains. "There's this one old babe, that every time I go there I have to knock on her door and tell her again who I am, 'cause she forgets. Else she calls the police," he told us.

He sat at the supper table with a stack of bread on a plate at his elbow and while he talked he buttered one slice after another flat on his hand and ate it. Grass-cutting was hard work. He felt the need to fortify himself. He told us about how, at one house, he'd sat on the front porch to eat his lunch. "The lady came out with a broom and started to sweep the porch like crazy," he said. "She got closer and closer to me and the grit was flying into my sandwich, which I'd put down on a piece of waxed paper beside me. Finally I turned to her and said, 'Excuse, me, ma'am? Would you like me to sit somewheres else to eat?' And she said, 'Now you mention it, I would. This ain't a park bench.'"

"Oh, Stirling, stop it!" Mom would beg from the end of the table, where she was holding her sides and laughing so hard the tears came out. "Stirling, you're making it up! Wait a minute while I catch my breath!"

Stirling sat there buttering his bread, full of himself but in a good way for once, just as surprised as the rest of us that he'd turned into our supper entertainment.

For the first time in my life it was a source of some pride to me to have a big brother and to be able to walk down a foreign street and see him in the yard of somebody I didn't even know, cutting their grass in a very profound and businesslike way, pushing the mower hard, a cigarette hanging out of his mouth. It gave me a strange feeling. One day, coming home from the confectionery with my new friend, Bonita Connor, I stopped and said, "That's my brother, Stirling," which was something I never wanted to admit before. She paused with a popsicle halfway to her lips, took a good look at him over a boxwood hedge and said, "No kidding," in a way that made me feel good.

One afternoon toward the end of July, Stirling pushed his lawn mower into Bonita's backyard. She and I were sitting on a blanket in the sun playing with her paper dolls.

"All right, children," Stirling said, "get off the lawn."

"I never knew you were cutting Bonita's grass," I said, surprised to see him there. The Connors had just moved into the neighbourhood that summer.

"New customer," said Stirling, bending over and taking a cookie out of a tin we had there with us on the blanket.

"Those aren't for you," I told him, but Bonita picked the tin up and held it out to Stirling.

"Have as many as you like," she said and he took a handful, more than I'd had myself.

"Aren't you girls a little old for dolls?" said Stirling. He was trying to look big in front of Bonita. I don't know why. She was homely. She had poached-looking skin, mauve lips, pink eyelids, hair almost white, not pretty. She made me think of a white rabbit.

Stirling bent over and jerked the starter cord. The roar of the mower drove us indoors. It was dark all the time in their house because Bonita's mother had the curtains drawn so she could watch television without the glare of the sunlight on the screen. She never came out of the living room to talk to us and we never went in.

148

From the hallway, I could barely make out her tiny figure, sitting in a big armchair, her hand curled around a glass on a side table. I'd begun to think of her as somebody who had floated out of the television itself, a blue, flickering, drowned figure. Bonita and I took the paper dolls upstairs to her room and sat on the bed, with the sound of Stirling's mower rising to us through the window screen. Once, I caught Bonita looking out the window and she said, "Your brother's cute."

I said, "Who, *Stirling*?"

After he'd gone away, we went outside again and tried to play but Bonita's heart somehow wasn't in it. Around five o'clock, her father, who managed the Metropolitan store, came home. We heard the *thunk* of his car door slamming and then we saw him come around the corner of the house. He always came to see Bonita before going inside. He was an extraordinarily tall and heavyset man, well dressed, with size twelve shoes, nice suits, and ties with pictures of Canada geese or racing cars or baseball players all over them.

"How are you girls? Did you get to the store today? Here's a dollar each. Go and buy yourselves something."

Bonita would pretend she didn't hear him and just go on playing even though he called her "my little white butterfly" and often had something for her from the store.

"Here, Bonita, I've brought you some sunglasses," he said one day, but Bonita didn't pay any attention even though he kept standing there, holding them out to her. They were beautiful too, turquoise with rhinestones in the corners. We were sitting on the ground and he was towering over us, throwing a long shadow between us, across the lawn. There was a terrible emptiness in the air while his hand hung there offering the sunglasses. I looked up at his big Irish face and I was torn by the bewilderment on it. It was more than I could stand. "Take them, Bonita," I finally said, so she took them all right and she threw them across the grass. Mr. Connor turned red and gave a little laugh. Then he went up the porch steps, took in a big gulp of air, like a swimmer about to plunge underwater, and opened the screen door.

After he was gone I said to Bonita, "What did you do that for?" But she just said, "Oh, never mind!" and her face was angry and sad.

I didn't understand Bonita and her family but I didn't want to figure them out. They were so unusual. I just liked to have the mystery of them sitting in my head, undisturbed, like something beautiful and uncommon resting on a shelf, something you don't know how it's made and you just don't want to know, you wouldn't take it down to find out because that might spoil its specialness, its magic.

---

In August, the heat waves came, the sidewalks shimmered, dogs crept in under the cool of porches. The sky got bigger and at noontime it burned like a furnace, yellow at its apex. It seemed there wasn't a sliver of shade to be had all day and everything looked harsh and sapped by the heat. The sun beat down and the grass jumped up out of the ground. Stirling would come down to breakfast and we could see from his face he'd been praying for rain so he could take a day off, but it never came, only brief showers at night, just enough to settle the dust, as Dad would say. Stirling couldn't get a rest from the lawn-cutting. Dad would elbow Stirling and say, "Gonna be another cooker. No rest for the wicked, eh, Stirling?" He was cheerful because he knew he'd been right about the weather, he was like a prophet. "Lawn mower's gonna be smokin', you're not careful," Dad told him.

Stirling was overworked but he seemed to have plenty of time to kill when it came to cutting the Connor yard. He'd find us sitting out on the blanket and say, "Move along, little girls," because he could see it infuriated Bonita.

"Don't call me that."

"What you want me to call you, then? Little queen? Queen Bonita? Will that do?" It was sickening, the way he talked.

Stirling's arrival interrupted Bonita's train of thought. She lost interest in playing. "It's too hot," she'd say to me. "I'm going into the house where it's cool."

"I'll come too," I'd say.

"No, I'm tired. I think I should lie down."

One day when I went to Bonita's she said, "I don't want to play paper dolls any more. You can have them for keeps if you want. I'm going downtown."

I went along with her even though she didn't invite me. At the Metropolitan store I watched her pick out a pair of nylon stockings, an eyebrow tweezer, a lipstick, a compact of clay-coloured face powder. She told the clerk, "Charge this to Mr. Connor." We passed the lunch counter on the way out. I said, "Let's have a Coke float," because I knew we could charge that too.

"No," said Bonita. "I'm too fat."

"Oh, Bonita!" I told her. "You are not. You're skinny as anything."

———————

With Bonita being tired and hot and headachy so many afternoons, I was spending more and more time at home. I went downstairs and found Dad working at the metal desk under a bare light bulb. I sat with my chin on my hands and watched him drawing. On the corner of the desk was a stack of finished diagrams. He let me look through them. They were done in heavy lead pencil, showing complicated interlocking wheel systems, belts, motors, pistons, carburetors, spark plugs. All the parts were neatly labelled. I read out loud: "Compression-ignition engine. Float pump. Camshaft. Universal joint. Flywheel. Differential."

Now and again, Mom would come downstairs to fetch something, the laundry or a jar of preserves. If Dad said to her, "Come

over here and look at this," she'd scowl and answer, "I'm busy working, as you can see. I haven't got time to look at pictures." Through
the openings in the stairs, we'd watch her go back up.

"Your mother has legs like stovepipes," Dad said once. Another
time he forgot to hide his whisky bottle and Mom noticed it at his
elbow. "I haven't got food to put on the table and you come up to a
meal with booze on your breath. I'd love to know where you hide
it," she said.

Later, around dinnertime, I'd find her sitting unhappily in the
kitchen, drawing circles over and over on the table with her index
finger.

———

On the last day in August, Dad and I were in the basement late in
the afternoon when the telephone rang upstairs. We heard the
basement door open and Mom called down in her stiff and digni-
fied company voice: "Farrel, it is Mr. Connor on the phone wanting to speak to you." Dad went upstairs, took the receiver from her
and sat down at the kitchen table. From the living room, Mom and
I listened.

"Yes, this is Stirling's father. Yes. Yes. When exactly was this?
You're sure about it? I understand. Yes, I realize it's a very serious
matter." His voice was meek, eager to please. "I'll certainly talk to
him. I'll do more than that, you can be sure. I promise you I'll follow it up. Thank you for calling. Thank you, Mr. Connor. It won't
happen again, don't you worry about that. Yes, it's unfortunate. No,
I don't. No, I agree, it should be kept quiet."

Dad hung up and from the living room I saw him look around
quickly, like someone waking up from a dream, and he said,
"Where's that goddamned Stirling?" After that, Mom and Dad
talked at length in their bedroom with the door closed.

At five thirty, Stirling came in with his chest bare and tanned and his shirt flung over his shoulder. Dad met him in the front hall. "You've cut your last lawn, my boy," he said. Then he opened the cellar door and pushed Stirling down there.

I went and sat on the floor in the living room where I knew Dad's and Stirling's voices would rise up to me through the furnace vent.

"We were only kissing. We weren't doing anything wrong."

"And her with all her clothes off."

"She took 'em off, not me."

"That's not what Mr. Connor said."

"Mr. Connor wasn't there. She was naked of her own free will."

"You must have had something to do with it."

"She wanted me up there."

"No decent girl wants that."

"How do you know she's decent?"

"Don't give me any of your lip."

Then Mom saw me there and knew what I was doing. "You come out here in the kitchen with me and help with dinner," she said.

That night, Stirling and I were upstairs, ready to go to bed. He hadn't spoken to me all evening, but before he went into his room he said to me, "I got something to show you. Take a look at this." He turned around and drew up his pajama top, showing me his back. There were welts all over it, bands of red from Dad's belt, some of which had been bleeding. I started to cry when I saw it and Stirling said, "Oh, shut up. You're such a crybaby. I don't know why I tell you anything." He laughed at me, angry and proud.

---

The next day, Stirling went out without telling anybody where he was going, and neither Mom nor Dad called after him to explain himself. Mom didn't talk much. I could see from her face that she was bursting with recent events and I knew all I had to do was chip away, chip away, and soon I'd have the whole story. All morning, I kept saying things like, "Stirling didn't look too happy when he went out," and "Dad is sure quiet downstairs," my voice calm and detached, as if I didn't really care.

What I finally got out of her was this: Every time Stirling went over to Bonita's to cut the grass, she went upstairs to her room, which overlooked the backyard. She took off her clothes and stood at the window bare naked until Stirling looked up and noticed her. After this happened a few times, Stirling got the idea that Bonita wanted him up there with her, so he slipped into the house through the back door. Mom didn't know the exact circumstances of Mrs. Connor's discovery of Stirling and Bonita: whether she found them after returning from the liquor store in a taxi and, seeing the lawn mower idle in the yard, traced Stirling to Bonita's room; or whether she heard something suspicious from upstairs while she was watching television and decided to investigate.

The longer I thought about it the easier it was for me to picture Stirling out in the August sun, bare-chested, pushing the mower around the lawn in smaller and smaller squares, at some point looking up, perhaps when he made a pivot, thinking the first time he noticed Bonita in the window that he had sunstroke, wiping the sweat out of his eyes and looking again. It did not stretch my imagination to think of Bonita standing in the window, her body, white as a slug, pressed against the screen, her breasts like small, firm, ripening apples, maybe her triangle showing too, above the windowsill, a thin and catlike smile on her face, and her mother downstairs with the television going full blast.

The day after the beating I didn't want to speak to Dad. I felt so ashamed of what he'd done to Stirling. And he might have been thinking himself that he'd gone too far because he went out before lunch in the car and Mom and I had to eat alone. During dessert, I said to her, "Dad hides his whisky bottle in the coal bin. He said you'd never look there."

Luckily, Dad never knew I told because that afternoon the coal man came. It was the first of September. Mom went down and opened the cellar window so that the man could fit the chute in. She put cloths over the heating vents upstairs, so that when the coal came thundering into the basement and a cloud of oily black dust boiled up and settled like ink over everything, including Dad's drawings, it did not ascend into the rooms upstairs.

After Mom let out the whole story about Stirling and Bonita, she looked relieved and guilty and she said to me, as though it was my fault she'd told, "I'm just telling you because I want you to realize what happens to girls like Bonita. You stay away from her."

But even if I'd wanted to stay friends with Bonita, I couldn't have because that fall at school she started to run with a wild gang that was loud and rebellious. They shouted in the halls and shoved each other and skipped classes in the middle of the day to go downtown and sit in the Metropolitan store smoking and drinking coffee. I wondered what Mr. Connor thought of that. Soon we heard that Bonita had gotten herself pregnant.

That fall, a change came over Stirling too. He went outside after supper to join the other boys on the street, grouped under a lamppost, laughing and smoking and avoiding homework, until long after the leaf rakers had gone inside and darkness had fallen.

Mom worried about Stirling out there. "Tell him to come in, Farrel," she said, but Dad told her, "Stirling's going to do what he's going to do. We can't stop him," and Mom sat in the kitchen and drew circles on the table.

It was as though the beating Stirling got from Dad was an initiation, a rite of passage, a coming-of-age, setting him free from Dad's power. I envied Stirling his newfound liberty, his deliverance from something I did not yet understand. I could not help but feel that the important events of the summer had somehow passed me over. I sensed that the grass-cutting, innocent as it seemed, had only been Stirling biding his time until something happened, some door opened and set him loose. Bonita, with her fruity breasts and enticing hips, with her body luminous and dreamy beyond the screen window, seemed to have been that door. I wondered if she had ever considered me a friend or if I'd been nothing more than a tool in her hands, an agent for her grand plot, a way of getting to Stirling. How gullibly I'd played along, sympathetic to her as she lay in bed on those hot afternoons with one of her headaches manufactured in order to get rid of me so she could display herself to Stirling.

Late in the afternoons when I was coming home from school, I sometimes saw Mr. Connor in his driveway, getting out of his car in one of his quality suits, a tragic and meticulous man. He would raise his hat and say, "Good afternoon, Marie. You are looking well. Fine October day," but I noticed a sadness and fixity in his smile, and when he turned and walked to the house his step was slower and less buoyant than before. I believed that he must have known, back on that day when Bonita threw the sunglasses across the yard, that the incidents of the summer and fall were going to unfold the way they did but he was helpless to stop them. It amazed me that such a tall, broad-shouldered man could be so powerless.

Sometimes in my dreams the image of Stirling's back, with its pattern of raised welts and blisters, flew up in my mind. And Dad too may have been haunted by the memory of the beating he gave Stirling. He didn't go back into the basement for a long time. He picked up a job again at the garage, working as a mechanic. He went back to calling Mom June, instead of speaking to her through me, as he'd done all summer.

One day, I was coming home from school and caught a glimpse of Bonita sitting on her back porch. Cautiously I walked down the driveway to the backyard.

"Bonita?" I said.

She jumped and turned around quickly, her expression not angry, as I'd feared it might be, but relieved.

"Oh, hello, Marie."

I went and sat beside her on the porch.

"I don't have any cookies to offer you," she said.

"That's all right."

She wore a loose cotton dress and a thin cardigan sweater, inadequate protection against the October wind. At our backs, the door stood open, Mrs. Connor's television entertainment drifting out to us through the screen. Bonita's hand rested on her stomach and I noticed there was an unnatural rise there. I hadn't seen her at school for a few weeks.

"You heard about my baby?"

"Yes."

"The whole town knows. Well, I don't care. What does it matter?"

"Will you stay here?"

"My father wants me to."

"That's nice of him, I guess."

"It's the least he can do."

"What do you mean?"

"This is his baby I got in my belly," she said. She saw the astonishment on my face. "Whose did you think it was? Stirling's?"

"I didn't know. No, I never thought it was Stirling's. I thought maybe one of your new friends."

"I should be so lucky," she said, and laughed bitterly.

Soon after this she ran away.

I wondered where she'd gone and if any of us would, like Bonita, break free of the conventionality of the street. Certainly Mr. and Mrs. Connor would not, nor would my father. And what about me? In revealing where my father's whisky bottle was hidden, I feared I'd shown my true colours, allied myself with my mother, who sat downstairs in the kitchen, trapped within the endless circles she drew on the table.

Autumn was drawing to a close. In the evenings I sometimes stood in my flannelette nightgown and looked out my window at the knot of boys standing in a cone of blue light. I listened to their explosive laughter and watched the red bonfires smouldering at the curbs, up and down the street.

# THE VIEW FROM HERE

I

AT NINE O'CLOCK in the morning, Dilys carries a sheaf of invoices down to Honora.

"Victor wondered if you could sort these for him," she says.

Honora is sitting at the hotel reception desk reading the newspaper. It's her job to answer the telephone, to check people in and out, to handle inquiries and small housekeeping problems raised by guests. However, these days the telephone does not ring very often, there is little traffic in the rooms or on the stairs, for it is the end of October, it is, in fact, Halloween. The tourist season has pretty well wound down, though there will be a flurry of activity at Christmastime, people escaping from the city, from Toronto mainly, to pass the holiday season here where there is no commercialism, where the climate is temperate, and where they can walk through the simple streets and down to the lake on Christmas Day to look at the cold charcoal water and the strange spectacle of the beach coated with a thin layer of snow, like almond icing on a fruitcake. Already the hotel is booked solid from December 24 to New Year's.

This morning it is grey and blustery, Honora's favourite kind of day, when business is slow and she can sit with her mug of coffee in

159

the little reception booth tucked under the stairs halfway down the dim, narrow hallway from the front door. She looks at magazines borrowed from the parlour, writes letters or makes personal telephone calls. Sometimes, as from a physical distance, she pictures herself sitting in the soft yellow wash of light from the little Tiffany lamp on the counter, inhabiting a warm, protected island at the heart of the dark, silent hotel.

"Don't bother with the invoices if you don't have time," says Dilys. Is there a touch of irony in her voice? wonders Honora. Probably. Honora knows that she doesn't do enough to make it worthwhile for Dilys to keep her on reception, but she doesn't offer to do any more. She is fifty and she is not interested in working, she has never been interested in working, but she is even less so now. From time to time Honora talks about moving back to the city because she knows it will throw Dilys into a panic. Five years ago, Dilys called Honora and asked her to come down here from Toronto to help out at the hotel. She had heard about Honora's divorce, she might even have been happy that it had freed Honora up to come to Franklin Bay. Honora and Dilys are cousins. They grew up together in the same wealthy Toronto district of stone houses, vast properties, topiary shrubs, iron fences. There were dozens of cousins in this neighbourhood, all private-schooled, uniformed, spoiled and petulant, but it was Honora that Dilys decided to latch on to.

"I can't stand being alone here with Victor," Dilys confessed when she was persuading Honora to come and work for her. "I love him but he bores me out of my mind. He has no sense of humour, no spark. He's a mole. I need you," she told Honora. "We're like sisters."

Dilys is with Victor because it is important for her to be married at this point in her life; she requires it in order to feel complete. Years ago, she led a wild life in Toronto with her first husband, who makes documentary films about artists, composers, dancers. She invested a good deal of her inheritance in these ventures and lost money. While Dilys was meeting with the bankers, trying to keep the film company afloat, her husband was conducting exhaustive research into a young ballerina. Dilys discovered them in bed together. After the split-up, Dilys was able to salvage something, she got enough money out to buy this small nineteenth-century hotel. She came here to Franklin Bay, a town of less than a thousand people, for a cure. Nobody who knew her was at all surprised. Dilys is a person of extremes, of dramatic swings of behaviour.

Out on the long two-storey porch, with its spindle banisters and curlicue brackets, the bales of hay and wheat sheaves and grape-vine wreaths blow in the wind. Tomorrow, when Halloween is over, Dilys will have these and the pumpkins she herself carved in intricate lace patterns removed. Soon she will be seen at a desk in one of the cozy lounges at either end of the central hall designing the Christmas decorations, inside and out, for the hotel: there will be big velvet bows, fir garlands, pine-cone wreaths, constellations of white lights everywhere.

While Victor has a good business head and is useful to Dilys for keeping the books balanced, it is she who has the style, the flair for décor, for drama and ambiance, that carries the hotel. The velvet wing chairs in the sitting rooms, the wooden decoys and carved pheasants, the gas fireplaces, rich wooden floors, snow shoes, Currier and Ives prints, gilt mirrors, scenic collectors' plates, lamps made out of antique water pumps were all her idea. In the guest rooms there are no telephones, the walls are pine or brick, the beds high and soft, with plain white coverlets. There is a simplicity to the place that Honora feels has a calculated, self-conscious quality, meant to appeal to big-city ideas of pure country life. For authenticity, Honora's own taste runs to seedy motels on deserted highways, broken mattresses, mildewed bathtubs.

Every year the hotel turns a bigger and bigger profit. With the exception of Honora, Dilys gets a lot out of her staff. She is not so much a good manager of people as someone who lashes out and pushes and bullies and shouts until she gets what she wants. Also, she has a talent for public relations. She has persuaded noteworthy people, Shakespearean actors, opera singers, broadcasters, to have their weddings here at the hotel, and got the stories covered by the Toronto papers. The hotel has been written up in all the right magazines. Dilys moved here, thinks Honora, because she wanted her own town. And it must be admitted that the hotel put Franklin Bay on the map. Dilys led the way, then other entrepreneurs followed, opening a coffeehouse, a scattering of bed and breakfasts, an English pub, boutiques selling designer T-shirts, native art, silver jewellery, pewter, English woollens, stained glass. People began to retire here, for the mild climate and the quaint shops on York Street with their picket fences and clapboard siding and Georgian windows.

Dilys leans over the counter. Everything about her appearance—the aubergine lipstick, the heavy biscuit face powder, the rhinestone frames of her glasses, the burgundy hair—everything is calculated to shock. She thinks of herself as a work of art, but the effect is not beautiful, it is bizarre, it borders on—well, on the Halloweenish. She is short and heavy and waddles a little when she walks. She has bad feet and must wear low shoes. In the thrust of her bosom, the circumference of her biceps, the span of her hands, the way she stands with her feet firmly planted apart like a heavyweight boxer, there is something solid, something threatening. Dilys is no pushover. She is a force to be reckoned with.

"Victor and I were down on the pier last night," she says meaningfully.

"Were you?" says Honora without interest.

"We passed your friend's boat."

"Oh?"

"The boat was rocking like crazy, Honora," says Dilys with mild disbelief, a touch breathless. "It was so obvious. People knew what was going on. Those curtains he has aren't entirely opaque. We could see shapes. We could see figures moving. We might have even heard some moaning."

"We're two consenting adults. We were doing it on private property."

"But, Honora! On the *pier*!"

"Nobody's forcing people to stop and look. Or to listen either."

Dilys sighs resignedly, perhaps a little listlessly. "What's it like with a younger man?" she asks, her face sagging with thinly disguised envy.

"It's kinky. It's like incest. Forbidden fruit."

"I thought you usually did it at your place. Why pick the boat?"

"Variety is the spice of life."

"It must be hard to do it in there. In the boat. With so little room. I suppose there's a bed of sorts, I suppose you do it on the bed."

"Never! Too dull, too comfortable."

"Where, then?"

"Sometimes he puts me up on the kitchen counter. He ties my hands behind me, to the faucet. He ties my ankles to the cupboard door handles. He puts a gag over my mouth. He blindfolds me. He starts with whatever instruments are within reach, smooth, fat wooden handles, empty beer bottles, a turkey baster, penetrating, teasing me until I'm nearly crazy." Honora is embellishing now because she knows Dilys wants it, needs it. "And the rocking, the rocking of the boat. It drives you mad. Things build quickly, with the motion. It's like riding a roller coaster with nothing on. It's like sitting naked on a magnificent, slowly galloping steed. Dilys, you just don't know."

Dilys presses her lips together for control, pulls on her trench coat, picks up her purse and keys. This morning she is making a trip up the lake to Goderich, where she is having a revised brochure printed up, with next summer's rates and new menus for the hotel dining room.

"Victor is feeling punky today," she confides in Honora. "He's more depressed than usual. He needs some sort of pick-me-up. Slip up and comfort him for a minute if you get the chance."

"I don't know if I'll have time. I have these invoices to sort."

"Oh, forget the invoices. It's bound to be slow at the desk today. Take a moment or two. I'll be gone all morning."

Honora knows what Dilys is talking about. Isn't Dilys always thrusting Honora and Victor together? Doesn't she put them in positions where there are opportunities for mischief, for compromise? She is always testing Honora. She is testing Victor. Placing them in such tableaux must give her a feeling of power. At the same time, she does not believe Honora would ever take advantage of such moments. She relies on Honora's loyalty, on her friendship.

Victor's office is on the second floor of the hotel. Sometimes his door is locked in the daytime. Dilys and Honora believe Victor masturbates up there. Dilys doesn't care what he does to himself. That's his business, she says. She finds Victor's sexual needs childish and pathetic. She has told him she won't have sex with him any more. Honora knows all of this because Dilys tells her everything. She talks about Victor as though he were a child and she a mother confiding her problems to another mother. She talks about him with much the same reckless candour and wounded pride with which Honora talks about her daughter, Rachel, who has recently followed Honora to Franklin Bay. Honora and Dilys have told each other too much in their lifetimes, so much that they could never afford to terminate their friendship. It would be dangerous, incriminating. There is a great deal at stake.

## II

After Dilys leaves, Honora picks up the telephone and dials Toronto. Dilys must know about these long-distance calls Honora places from the hotel desk but she never mentions them.

"Hello, Mother."

"Who is this?" comes a small, hostile voice.

"It's Honora."

"You never call me."

"I'm calling you now. I called you last week." As she speaks, Honora is picturing the quiet treed streets, the circular driveways, the tennis courts of her childhood neighbourhood, where her mother continues to live. She still has a good deal of money, but is stingy about giving any of it to Honora. To get anything out of her, Honora must pay somehow, she must make these phone calls, she must put up with the abuse.

"I'm aching everywhere and nobody cares," says her mother petulantly.

"You should get out of bed occasionally."

"It's cozy under the covers. It's raining here."

"You should be up walking. You take too many pills."

"I love my pills. I love the colour of them. I have every colour in the rainbow."

"But, Mother, you don't need medication. There's nothing wrong with you."

Honora's mother has always been a hypochondriac. From the earliest Honora can remember, everything in the house had to revolve around her mother. She never cooked Honora a meal in her life. There was a housekeeper. Honora's mother stayed in bed and bullied Honora's father until it killed him. He was a meek, kind and tolerant man, a professor of mathematics at the university. When he came home from his classes in the evening, he carried bowls of soup up to her bed, laid out clean nightgowns for her, brushed her long hair. He tended to her needs with the orderliness, the pragmatism, the attention to detail of a mathematician.

"What about *me*?" Honora had asked him.

"Of course I love you too," he told her, but Honora believed that if he'd really loved her, he would have taken her away from her mother and let her have a childhood. When he died, Honora's mother did not attend the funeral.

"I'm too exhausted," she said from her bed. At the burial site, Honora picked up a handful of earth. It was a dry, loose, infertile soil. When she tossed it on the coffin, much of it blew away in the wind. What a fool you were, Father, she thought. What a waste you made of your love.

"I saw Ford's picture in the news today," says Honora's mother.

Ford, Honora's ex-husband, is a criminal lawyer who has his name in the papers all the time. He defends famous white-collar murderers, often businessmen, accused of committing clean, brilliant, innovative crimes.

"It was the society column. He goes to all the best functions."

"That would impress you."

"Why did you have to move to Franklin Bay?"

"I like the view from here, Mother."

"If you came back to Toronto," says Honora's mother, "I'd give you money."

"You never gave me money before, when I lived there. Actually, Mother, now that you mention it, I could use a little help right now."

"You shouldn't need my money, at your age. If you hadn't thrown away all your opportunities. Your father and I wanted everything for you. You could have gone to university. You had the brains. You could have gotten an arts degree, like Dilys. But you ran away to Europe. I felt so betrayed."

"Mother, that was thirty years ago."

"You didn't call us for months on end."

"I needed space, Mother."

"You lived in some slum."

"It was a flat. There was nothing squalid about it."

Honora's mother doesn't know the half of it. When she was twenty, Honora was working in Madrid for a photographer. She grew up overnight. She tried marijuana and cocaine. She learned to masturbate. She slept with the photographer and found that she

did not feel guilty about his wife Rosaria and their little son Jesus.
The photographer paid her very little and, as he neared bankruptcy,
nothing at all. After a year, Honora came back to Canada because
her parents refused to send her any more money and because, returning one day to the studio with sandwiches and a bottle of wine,
she found the photographer naked on top of a client on the floor, all
tangled up among the extension cords and electrical wires. Back in
Canada, Honora met, in her parents' house, Ford, a law student
and the son of an academic colleague of her father. She married
him. At the time, it seemed the easiest thing to do.

"Dilys was here to visit—oh, two weeks ago," says Honora's
mother.

"I know. I sent my love through her."

"She's such a faithful niece. Such original ideas. That is the kind
of daughter I wanted. People like Dilys make things happen. She
talked about you." Honora recalls Dilys's words when she set off for
the visit. "I'll put in a good word for you," she promised Honora.

"She's so protective of me," Honora says.

"Protective! Ha! Don't you know, Honora? Don't you realize
that Dilys resents you in so many ways? She says you're passive and
lazy."

"You don't know that."

"She didn't want to say it but I got it out of her. We had a long
heart-to-heart talk. She called you a freeloader. Don't tell her I told
you."

After she hangs up, Honora bites the inside of her cheek until it
bleeds. How alike are Dilys and Mother, thinks Honora for the first
time: the envy, the nastiness, the blame. What has Honora done to
threaten Dilys? Is it her long legs? Her deep, gravelly voice? The
tranquil core of her that Dilys has said she so admires? Her Chanel
suits left over from her life with Ford? The class she gives the reception desk, which is exactly what Dilys said the hotel needed? Honora looks out the hotel window at leaves blowing down the street, at

stores across the way, many of them closed up already for the season; most will not reopen even for Christmas, their owners have gone off to Florida or Australia for the winter. Soon Franklin Bay will resemble a ghost town. Honora feels a wave of something. Sadness? Panic? Once again, she sees herself sitting in the little reception cubicle, a bird in a bright cage. For a moment, she feels she would like to tear the hotel down, board by board.

She sets about sorting the invoices. It is not so big a job after all, it takes less than half an hour. When she begins her hands are shaking, but by the time she finishes the shaking has stopped because she knows what she must do. She gathers the invoices together, lifts a section of the counter, slips through and lowers it again. Quietly, she makes her way upstairs, passing the restaurant, with its orange tile floor and Shaker chairs and stiff white napkins folded like swans and long fan-shaped windows giving a view of the street. Distant, muted sounds of cooking come from the kitchen, the smell of onions frying. Honora treads softly on the deep stair carpet. Turning at the top step, she goes down the narrow, deserted hallway, which is filled with the salty smell from the sauna at the end of the passage. She knocks gently on Victor's door, looks quickly up and down the hall, then slips swiftly inside.

He is sitting in an old, heavy swivel desk chair, wearing his customary three-piece tweed suit—it is a kind of uniform for him, his suit of armour, you might say, protecting him, if that is possible, from Dilys's scrutiny, from her harping. Through the window, a pearl light falls on his long, almond-shaped head, which is bald and shiny and somewhat pointed on top, like a very large, smooth and absurd bird's egg.

"Honora—?" he turns to her, nonplussed. Even after all these years he is shy, surprised around her, perhaps because she and Dilys have such a solid history together, a good chunk of Dilys was already spoken for, before Victor ever met her. He cannot help feeling like a latecomer, a gate-crasher, a third party.

"I've brought you something, Victor," Honora says. He reaches out to take the invoices. "No, not these," she says, and lets them flutter to the floor. She grasps the back of his chair and turns him around so that the window is behind him. The room is hot, she can smell his stale suit. Reaching down, she loosens his tie.

"Honora, what—?"

Unfastening his belt, she pulls his trousers, his underwear down over his white hips, over his hairy knees, lets them fall in a tangle around his ankles, onto his heavy-stitched Oxford shoes, so that he could not get up and flee even if he'd wanted to. Even if he'd wanted to. Honora doesn't feel anything like surprise at what she's undertaken, but goes about her task with a certain economy, with rapid, deft movements. Perhaps she has imagined this scene before, perhaps she has dreamt it.

Is this survival? wonders Honora, looking out the window over Victor's head as she moves on top of him, causing his chair to glide pleasantly, rhythmically, on its wheels. Or is it destruction? What does she want? Is she striking out at the alliance between her mother and Dilys? Is she trying to chip away a little piece of Dilys's establishment, attacking at its foundations? The rough wool of Victor's suit jacket burns her knees. She unbuttons her blouse but he does not dare to touch her skin. Victor is terrified of Honora. He is terrified of Dilys. He only looks at her bare breasts, her navel, the curve of her hips revealed by the loosened blouse. His hands rest, as though they are dead, on the chair arms. He is like a little cringing dog, thinks Honora with disgust. Out of him comes a whimper, helplessness, gratitude, begging her not to stop, but to carry them all the way.

What a pathetic ruin he is, Honora thinks, an empty, quaking shell, hollowed out by Dilys, blasted powdery as ash by her temper, by the sheer force of her will. But aren't they both damaged? Aren't they, together, Honora and Victor, the wreckage from Dilys's ambitions? What I am doing, thinks Honora, will cause problems for

Victor, problems for Dilys, somewhere down the road. That is enough for me. It is not power she wants. No, the whole idea of power bores her. Rather, she is interested in lies and secrets, broken vows, taboos, sins, betrayals, violations, lust, damage, forbidden pleasures: what she sees as the true undercurrent of life, the dark web of desire, the private deeds meshed together, woven like horny undergarments, worn close to the body, that make the ordinary outward trappings, the apparel of everyday life supportable.

Afterward, Honora moves to the office door. Victor has tucked his shirt back into his pants, straightened his tie, mopped the perspiration from his scalp. He is on his hands and knees collecting the scattered invoices.

"Shall we tell Dilys about this?" Honora asks him.

"Christ, no!" he says, his face flushing with alarm.

"She might like to know. She might be relieved it's finally happened. Another item she could cross off her agenda. She's been pushing us together for a long time, hasn't she? She's been asking for this." If Honora were to tell her, Dilys would blame Victor. Honora and Victor both know this. She would be more likely to punish Victor than Honora. Blood is thicker than water.

"For god's sake, Honora, don't tell her! Jesus!"

### III

Dilys is gone for more than the morning. She does not return until two, her hair wild and her face ruddy from the wind. She comes to Honora before even taking her coat off.

"I saw Rachel," she says breathlessly. "When I got back into town I needed to go to the hardware store, so I had to drive down Louisa Street, past Holmes's clinic. Honora, I drove past and there she was in the goddamn window, hugging him in plain view. What on earth is she thinking of?"

"She's young."

"She's over twenty. She should behave more responsibly."

Dilys is not really one to talk about responsibility in children, thinks Honora. Dilys's daughter Euphemia is living in some sort of commune in Alberta, some sort of crazy religious camp. She has had three babies, all by different men in the commune. She is not even sure which men they were. The people in this commune, the men and the women, look very much the same, they look like sexless acolytes, with their flowing India cotton gowns, long matted hair, unwashed limbs, bead necklaces, thick leather sandals. There are apparently drugs in this community, and nudity, incense burning, trances, chants and rituals carried on by candlelight or by the illumination of the full moon. There may even be guns. Dilys flew out there once, hoping to talk sense into Euphemia, to bring her home. She came back shocked and totally disgusted. The commune, she said, was full of dirty cross-eyed children. She doesn't talk about Euphemia now. It is as if she never had a daughter.

"It's getting too overt," says Dilys about Rachel's behaviour. "Franklin Bay is a tiny community. People are conservative, they talk. If it gets out, the whole place could blow up over it."

"So be it."

"It could affect the hotel."

"People in Franklin Bay don't stay at the hotel."

"But they'd talk. They'd find ways to undermine, to sabotage."

"I'd leave then, if I proved a liability."

"But that's not the point!"

IV

Honora walks home through the town in the mellow afternoon light. It has been a warm and rainy fall. The last of the leaves have finally been torn from the trees, they are plastered flat to the wet pavement, like extinguished flames; they lie in pools of gold on front lawns, where the grass, uncut since September, is long and wet. It is a soft and agreeable afternoon, tinged with the not unpleasant sense of sadness and termination that autumn brings. The streets are pungent with the perfume of death, of the slow and steady disintegration of matter, the deep rotting smell of composting leaves, of fermenting apples lost in long grass, of branches knocked down by gusty winds to turn soft and slippery as snakes in the gullies, of the funky scent of toadstools and rich damp earth. Everywhere, on porches, in front windows, bedroom windows, is the droll burlesque of Halloween, pumpkins and paper witches and tissue ghosts, vain attempts to stir up a little horror. On one lawn, a dozen little skeletons, swinging from the branches of a crab apple tree, act out a strange and ghoulish comedy.

When Honora arrives home, Rachel is in the kitchen eating a grilled-cheese sandwich. Honora is surprised to see her there so early. This is usually the time of day when she plays her little games with Dr. Holmes, once the patients, the therapist, the bookkeeper have cleared out and before he must go home to his wife.

Honora goes down the narrow hall to the bathroom to freshen up, to give Rachel a little space. She and Rachel tread carefully around each other, they have learned there are regions that are off-limits. There is a fragility, a potential explosiveness to their relationship that has to do with Ford and with why they are both here in Franklin Bay. Rachel knows about Ford's infidelity. She knows the reasons that Honora and Ford are not together any more. She may understand them ideologically, but on an emotional level she is still angry. She will always be a child, in this sense, and she will always blame Honora because it is easier to blame the gender you know than the gender you don't. In the end, thinks Honora, women will always turn on each other like angry dogs.

Rachel went to university in Toronto and dropped out in the spring of her third year. She came here to live with Honora. She lay on the beach all summer and toward the end of August, when the weather grew cooler, she got this job, as the chiropractor's receptionist. Since nearly the first day, since Labour Day, she's been involved with Dr. Holmes. There is a big wire cage in the office, in the physiotherapy area, a section of curtained-off beds, with ropes and sturdy leather straps hanging from it. These are used to support injured limbs, mending hips and fractured arms that need traction and therapy. Rachel has told Honora about how Dr. Holmes puts her in this cage, ties her up, straps her down, whips and spanks and twists and drives her to a climax. Honora is fascinated and disgusted by these stories and also slightly incredulous. She finds it somewhat difficult to picture the shy and introverted, the thin, poker-straight and conservative-looking Dr. Holmes, with his serious face and his short grey military haircut, as a kind of circus ringmaster with a whip, a cruel gamekeeper in a zoo. On the other hand, she is able to believe Rachel's stories entirely, because she has learned that people are usually just the opposite of what they appear.

"He's sick. What he does to you is sick," says Honora.

"What you and Dennis do is sick."

"How would you know?"

"After I go to bed, Mother, don't you think I can hear things?"

Rachel tells Honora that she is going to meet Dr. Holmes at the office after dark. His wife will be busy at the house with the local children knocking on doors looking for Halloween treats. Dr. Holmes has told her he is going to a professional meeting up in Goderich.

"She's stupid enough to believe that," Rachel says smugly.

"Rachel, I doubt if Mrs. Holmes is stupid. She's a very successful business woman."

Rachel has been pressing Dr. Holmes to make a commitment to her. She wants him to get rid of Mrs. Holmes, she wants to live among the antiques in the sand-brick house on the cliff, the two-hundred-year-old house with the large grounds covered now with fallen oak leaves rich as copper shavings in the sun, and the converted brick butter-house where Dr. Holmes parks his Mercedes, where the wind is always blowing and the lake, far below, rises and falls like a sleeping giant.

"But the house is hers, don't you see that?" says Honora. "She must have family money."

"Peter has a thriving business," argues Rachel. "He has clients coming in from all over the county."

"You don't get rich, not that kind of rich, from cracking people's backs. And he won't want to give up his Mercedes."

"She can move out. She can go back to Toronto."

"Rachel, how do you think this is going to happen? She has the antique store. He has his business. Their livelihoods are here. People don't throw that away overnight. Neither of them will want to leave, and in a town this size they'd see each other every day. *You'd* see her."

"I don't care."

"Don't push it, Rachel. These things have a way of blowing up in a person's face."

"I refuse to be like you. I'm not going to settle for too little. I'm determined to be happier than you've ended up."

V

After Rachel leaves, the phone rings. It's Dennis. "Meet me down on the beach in half an hour," he says.

"Why not my place?" Honora asks.

"Too predictable."

"We'd have it to ourselves. Rachel's just gone out."

"Fucking the good doctor?"

"The beach will be cold."

"We'll build a fire. Even without the fire, you won't be cold. I'm going to do things to you that you'll never forget."

On a small dead end, where the houses are sparse, Honora takes a steep wooden stair down the cliff to the beach. She steps down onto the sand, her heart pounding even before Dennis moves out, swift as a deer, from behind a bush.

"Scare you?" he grins hopefully. He has told Honora he is in love with her, he wants to marry her, but she just laughs at him.

"You are inappropriate for me in every way," she has had to explain to him over and over. She met him a year ago when he docked his boat in Franklin Bay and started working at odd jobs down at the marina, repairing and maintaining people's boats. When he comes to Honora, he smells of the fishy lake, of outboard motor fuel, of strong oil-based paint, and this excites her. So do his youth, his lack of education, his irreverence, his physical strength, his leathery, prematuraly lined face. In his brief life, he has drunk heavily and done a lot of cocaine. He has had gonorrhea.

Now he leads Honora along the sand, which is firm and packed from the week's rains. As it turns out, Dennis becomes too excited to stop and gather the necessities for a fire, though there are branches strewn all over the beach from storms. His mouth is on Honora's neck, his hands are all over her body, sliding down her breasts, down her hips, pulling away her trench coat, yanking up her skirt, wrenching her stockings, her underpants without any regard for tearing them. This is what Honora wants from him: madness, violence, damage. He pushes her down on the beach, leaping on top of her like a wild cat. She pretends to object. He grabs her long hair in one hand and jerks her head around painfully. He kneels on one of her wrists, pressing it into the sand, takes ahold of the other and twists her arm behind her. He has got his pants down and has entered her, thrusting and grunting. Now Honora gives herself up to him entirely, abandons everything, feels her lower regions swollen with desire, need, longing, a rush of excitement flashes up through her body, as though the whole lake, lapping within earshot, has entered her loins to

175

flow upward. Finally, Dennis falls on her, his head pressed into the sand.

For a few moments, Honora lies there quietly, gazing up at the starry night and thinking: What is sex about, but self-destruction? This is what we all want, isn't it, to annihilate ourselves? In being subsumed by your partner, you become less, not more, you enter a black vacuum, like Alice falling down the hole.

Three-quarters of an hour later, Honora and Dennis are climbing back up from the beach when they see a powerful flashlight shining at the top of the stairs. The beam draws a circle, then floods down the steps, picking them out. They hear the clatter of urgent footsteps coming down toward them. Honora sinks down onto a bench built into the side of the stairs, halfway up. A police officer stops in front of her. There is another one further up. The flashlight shines in her face. She shields her eyes. She knows she must look a mess. Her hair is matted with sand, her trench coat is wet and soiled. The officer must wonder what they were doing down there. He must know. As soon as she saw the flashlight and heard the heavy boots on the stairs, Honora knew what was wrong.

"Are you Honora Gilchrist?" the officer asks her. He is not from Franklin Bay. There is no police force here, there is no crime. "It's about your daughter. I'm sorry to have to tell you that she's dead. It looks like murder."

## VI

Dilys says, "I saw him buying the gun. On Halloween day. It was when I went to Goderich to the printer. You know that gun shop out on Twenty-one just before the Clinton turnoff? Of course I didn't actually *see* the gun, but he was coming out of the shop with a box in his hand. That must have been the day he bought it. I didn't want to tell you this."

Yes, you did, thinks Honora. She is sitting at the reception desk stuffing flyers into envelopes. It is a week after the murder. This morning when Honora was walking to work, the first sweet and gentle snowflakes of the season started to fall. They came down softly, individually, like the picturesque and somehow unreal, the decorative snowfalls you see in Japanese prints. Honora came into the hotel with a light skin of white on her hair.

"Oh, Honora, don't you see? I could have prevented the murder!"

"But he didn't use the gun. He didn't use the gun on her. He used his bare hands."

"But if I'd called the police, they could have arrested him right then and there."

"They don't arrest a person for buying a gun. He had a permit." Honora knows all the details. She knows more about Peter Holmes now than she'd ever wanted to. Possibly, she now knows more about him than she ever knew about Rachel, her own daughter. It was in all the papers for a week, article after article. It seemed there was a dearth of excitement and gore in these parts. When it happened, people wanted to hold on to it as long as they could. Her first day back on the job, Honora had sat down at the reception desk and found a newspaper Dilys had placed there surreptitiously, with a big article about the murder.

"Oh, Honora," Dilys said later, that first morning, feigning surprise, feigning concern. "Are you reading that? How did that paper get there? Give that to me. You shouldn't have to see these things." Honora thinks that Dilys likes to believe she could have stopped the murder. It gives her some sort of power over Honora to believe this, an actual hand in her destiny. Dilys in fact learned of Rachel's murder before Honora did. The police, called to investigate Dr. Holmes' clinic after a neighbour reported hearing the discharge of a gun, then went for information to Dilys' hotel, it being the only establishment open on Halloween night. Dilys sent the police looking for Honora and Dennis down on the beach. Honora wonders if Dilys is pleased by the publicity of the murder, for might it not draw morbid sightseers—potential hotel guests—to Franklin Bay?

# VII

Honora's mother came to the funeral. Dilys drove down to Toronto and brought her up for it.

"I felt I had to, Honora," Dilys explained. "She called and asked me. What could I say?" You brought her because you wanted to undermine me, thinks Honora.

At the funeral, Dilys and Honora's mother sat shoulder to shoulder in a pew near the back of the church. Honora's mother looked jaundiced. She'd dug out her old mink cape with the mean, desiccated mink head on the collar, glaring up at her face.

"The smell of mothballs! I thought I'd keel over!" Dilys later confessed and Honora felt a strange twinge of hurt, on her mother's behalf, which surprised her.

"Aren't you angry?" Dilys demands, the day of the first snowfall. "Aren't you angry about the murder? Don't you have the courage to be angry? That was your daughter. Your flesh and blood."

"I know what a daughter is," says Honora. Honora believes that Dilys is in one respect happy about Rachel's death, because it has left Honora childless, much like Dilys herself, for Euphemia might as well be dead. All the other betrayals by Dilys, the control and the duplicity, Honora can tolerate. But this she cannot accept. "I know what a daughter is," she repeats. "When Rachel was alive, she loved me. You can't say that much for Euphemia."

Dilys goes away angry. Honora knows that there will now be consequences, as there have been following past disputes, past fallings-out between them. A lengthy period of coldness between Honora and Dilys will ensue. They will pass each other in the narrow hallways of the hotel looking the other way. They will speak only when business requires it. For a time, this will be all right with Honora. She will welcome the unfamiliar silence, being sick of Dilys's constant chatter. Honora will bide her time. She won't give in. She is a person who doesn't apologize. Oh, yes, she has made mistakes in her life, but they were part of her and she never backs down from them. Then one day Honora and Dilys will start talking again, because that is the way of families. It will have nothing to do with forgiveness or love. Honora will speak to Dilys because Dilys spoke to her. Or it may be the other way around. No one will keep track, no one will want to remember.

Now, Honora looks out at the shut-up stores across the street, which are softened, remote behind the white screen of snow. She wonders if this virgin snowfall will kill her, if it will destroy her with its gentleness, if the mild winter ahead, too kind after the death of Rachel, will finish her off for good.

Out on the street, the chiropractor's wife, Gillian Holmes, passes by on her way to her shop. She is carrying on with her antique business, just as before. A few days ago, she stopped Honora in the street, looking very cheerful in a smart red suit, black patent pumps, her cap of blondish hair shining in the sun.

"I'm sorry about your daughter," she said, surprising Honora.

"But you realize," said Honora, "that she was—?"

"Involved with Peter? Oh, yes. I'd known all along. However, there was no point in trying to stop it. You see, my husband was a very sick man. A violent man. He'd been in treatment several times. It's all very sad."

Dennis had not wanted Honora to visit the scene of the crime. She'd asked the police to take her there and he'd gone along, trying to dissuade her. When they reached the chiropractor's office, he'd put his hand on her arm.

"Honora, don't go in. Take their word for it," he said, but she shook his hand off angrily.

"I have to do this," she said. "I have to see it for myself. Leave me alone. Get your hands off of me!" And she went on in.

"Fuckin' bitch," Dennis said to her back.

In Dr. Holmes's office, Honora saw Rachel hanging upside-down like a carcass in the wire cage, bound there by leather straps, wearing only black underwear. Her neck had been broken but there were no marks on her body. After killing her, Dr. Holmes had lain down on the treatment table next to her and shot himself in the head. It all looked carefully planned and neatly executed, except, of course, for the doctor's blood sprayed against the walls and the partitioning curtains.

During the few days of compassionate leave that she took, Dennis came to Honora's house several times, but she would not answer the door. He began to drop off notes.

*Dear Honora,*
*I didn't meen nothin when I said that to you. It just come out*
*spontanius. It didn't have nothin to do with my jenuin feelings for*
*you as a woman and as a person . . .*

*Dear Honora,*
*Come to think of it maybe I did meen it when I called you a fuckin*
*bitch cause you've always been a helluva lay and not many women*
*your age can screw like you. So you shoulduv took it as a*
*complament. The above is ment as a joke a little humour whitch*
*I'm sure you could use some of . . .*

*Dear Honora,*
*I was a little coked up that night on the beach. I never told*
*you cause I didn't have enough stuff for both of us. It was*
*just something give to me for a favor I did a guy. So I got an*
*excuse for what I said to you. So will you take that into*
*consideration?*

*Dear Honora,*
*I love you.*

## VIII

Honora does not believe there is any such thing as love. Peter Holmes had said he loved Rachel, hadn't he, and he'd killed her? What, then, was the difference between love and hate? Honora thinks about her father. Even his love for her mother was, in the end, something else, wasn't it? Negotiation. Manipulation. Control. Codependence. Had Rachel loved Honora? Had Honora ever taught Rachel how to love? Honora cannot remember.

Honora heard that Dennis had left Franklin Bay. Dilys told her this. Didn't Dilys hear everything? Of course, Dilys was privately happy that he was gone. No longer would she have to worry about walking down on the pier some soft evening, passing Dennis's boat and knowing that Honora was in there, riding with pleasure on a slippery maple spoon handle.

Honora sits at her kitchen table after work. The image of Rachel hanging upside-down in the cage flashes up in her mind, choking her with grief, with the futility and valuelessness of everything. She sees Rachel's eyes, frozen in the moment of her death, so wide open and intense, staring at her, at the policeman, with the most compelling expression of—what? Astonishment? Horror? Fear? Regret? No. None of these. *Accusation.*

She goes to her bedroom, pulls out suitcases, begins to pack her clothes.

She is not sure exactly how she failed Rachel but she knows that she did. In some way she is responsible for Rachel's death. She did not set an example. She did not show Rachel how to live happily. She did not present her with an alternative to life with Peter Holmes. Perhaps Honora should never have left Ford. She should have stuck with him, as her own father had stuck with her mother, and that might have saved Rachel's life.

Honora cleans out the drawers of her bureau. Where will she go now? She remembers something her father once said to her.

"Honora," he said, "life is like mathematics. Whenever you make a mistake, when you find that your solution is wrong, you must go back to the beginning." Honora will return to Toronto now. She will start all over. She will try once more to make her mother love her.

As she is completing her packing, Honora comforts herself with one thought: perhaps Rachel had loved her after all. Perhaps that expression of hers when she died was a private message for Honora, a generous parting gift. *Watch out, Mother, watch out. You are in greater danger of self-destruction than you know.*

# STROKE

MRS. HAZZARD'S HUSBAND has been taken by ambulance to the hospital and now she has been allowed upstairs to see him. She finds their physician standing beside the bed in a cool glass-walled room. He is a lanky seven-foot man who dresses in heavy tweed suits like a country doctor. Mrs. Hazzard and her husband have always shared a belief that the doctor's height endowed him with extraordinary powers, but here among these machines and wires and beeping monitors he seems shockingly weakened, diminished, like a fallen god. For five years he has been pressing his stethoscope with his long beautiful fingers to their faulty hearts and talking to them in his grave respectful voice. But he never said things would come to this. This is not heart. Has someone played a trick on them all?

"Mr. Hazzard, you have had a stroke!" the doctor shouts so loudly that it startles Mrs. Hazzard. "Mr. Hazzard, you have had a stroke. Can you hear me? Do you understand?"

Mr. Hazzard opens his mouth eagerly to speak, but all that comes out is *jabber jabber jabber*. Mrs. Hazzard begins to cry.

"Now, now," says the doctor, laying a long hand on her shoulder. She cannot believe its terrible weight. She is certain it will crush her. He explains how strokes occur, how there is a blockage somewhere, an absence of blood supply, killing brain cells, which may or may not be replaced. Mrs. Hazzard cannot comprehend what he is

183

saying. It is both too simple and too complicated an explanation. In the doctor's blue eyes is something deeper, some dark knowledge for which she is not ready. She senses that he is preparing to abandon her and Mr. Hazzard. Already, he seems to have retreated from them a measurable distance. His kind smile pains her. He rushes off to another part of the hospital. Mrs. Hazzard would like to run away too but she must stay here, where nurses in dazzling white uniforms pad efficiently from room to room in their crêpe-soled shoes. All the patients here are very sick. Mr. Hazzard is no more important or lucky than any other. This thought frightens Mrs. Hazzard. Dusk is falling. She sees herself and her husband reflected against the black window like two silent actors on a bright stage.

———————

Mrs. Hazzard is calling her daughter Merilee far away in a part of the United States where there is never any snow. A male voice answers the phone. When Merilee comes on, Mrs. Hazzard asks, "Who was that?"

Merilee says coldly, "Just a friend." Mrs. Hazzard wonders if Merilee will marry this one. Merilee has had four husbands and is not yet thirty-five. Once, Mr. Hazzard asked her if she was trying to set some kind of record. They have not met the last three husbands and this has made it easier for them because they have been able to think of these men as thin characters in a series of entertaining American films. In these films love is amusing and not to be taken seriously.

Mrs. Hazzard tells Merilee what has happened to her father. Merilee asks her a string of questions to which Mrs. Hazzard may as recently as yesterday have had the answers but now cannot remember them.

"I'll call the hospital," says Merilee.

"Oh, I wish you wouldn't," says Mrs. Hazzard. "They're doing everything they can." Merilee has a way of destroying things. Mrs. Hazzard has a superstitious fear that a call from Merilee might trigger something. At the moment everything is in delicate balance, like a feather poised on a fingertip. One puff of air could send it spinning.

"Should I come home now? I don't want to come home now," says Merilee. "I'm going crazy. I haven't made my monthly quota." Merilee has quit nursing and is now selling cosmetics for a big company. She has an expense account and a company car, a small white convertible. Mrs. Hazzard pictures Merilee driving in this convertible through the hot yellow palm-lined streets of a southern city, wearing dark glasses and a short skirt. Merilee has bleached her hair and fixes it in a cumbersome Dolly Parton style. She diets until she has the waistline of a little girl. She has had breast implants, a face-lift, an abortion. Of course, Mrs. Hazzard finds all of this disturbing.

Merilee herself is sick enough to be in the hospital. She has nervous rashes, a stomach ulcer. She is like a gypsy, moving from one apartment to another, one husband to another. She can't sit still or be alone for more than five minutes. "You are running away from yourself," they have told her, but she laughs, her face, caked with heavy orange makeup, breaking into cracks.

"You sound more Canadian every day," she has told them. "I'll never come back to Canada. Nothing there is worth what you pay for it."

Now, Merilee tells Mrs. Hazzard, "I'd rather come near the end."

"Near the end of what?" asks Mrs. Hazzard. "Near the end of the month?"

"No," says Merilee. "If Dad gets worse, I mean. I'd rather come closer to the end. It costs so much to fly up there."

---

It is a sunny afternoon and Mrs. Hazzard is walking to the hospital, a journey of approximately one mile, taking her down a gentle hill, over a thin fall of fresh snow. She walks cautiously, afraid of falling. She passes an elementary school. It is recess and the playground is swarming with noisy children. Mrs. Hazzard stops on the sidewalk to look at the children, amazed. What vitality! What wonderful chaos! She is joyous and grateful for the sight of the children, for the beautiful day, for the white roads and lawns, for the knowledge that Mr. Hazzard has been taken off intravenous. The tubes and wires are gone and so is the catheter but he is wearing a big adult diaper. Several times a day, his cold fingers close with great urgency on Mrs. Hazzard's wrist. She listens expectantly. He pushes his face close to hers and says, "See, I can't . . ." or "I want . . ." but that is as far as he can get. She can feel the pressure of the message trapped in his head, pushing like water behind a dam, bursting to break through. He does not like to look at her. When he does, his eyes are full of a sorrow so devastating that even Mrs. Hazzard, with a voice still at her command, could not have found words to describe it.

"What do you want?" she gently encourages him. "What do you want? Tell me."

"He says what sounds like *kitchen kitchen kitchen*. He draws a U shape over and over on the table in front of him.

"A letter? The letter U?" Mrs. Hazzard guesses. "A cup? A curved road?" Mrs. Hazzard cannot understand. Mr. Hazzard pushes her away angrily.

"Ge out!" he shouts at her. "Ge out!" She blinks at him, a frozen smile on her face.

Later she walks in the hallway. This is a noisy, dirty part of the hospital. She does not like it here. After the bright and modern intensive care unit, this ward is wretched and grey. The nurses seem to be very angry. Mrs. Hazzard feels tension in the air. She wonders how a person is supposed to recuperate in such an environment. Surely this is not a healthy place!

"Will you bring my husband another blanket?" she asks a nurse. "It's so cold in this part of the hospital and the blankets are so thin."

"We can't be running after every little whim of the patients," the nurse tells her.

At dinnertime, tall, rattling trolleys are wheeled past the door and the smell of canned gravy fills the ward. A tray is brought in and placed on a table in front of Mr. Hazzard. Mrs. Hazzard lifts the stainless steel lids to reveal bowls of soft pale food. Mr. Hazzard stares down at the meal, uncomprehending. She gives him a cup of mushroom soup and he tries to drink it, using the hand that is not paralysed. The white soup runs in two rivers out of the corners of his mouth and down his chin. It gushes out his nose. Mrs. Hazzard takes the cup away from him. She feeds him small bites of custard with a child's spoon. He swallows with great gravity and concentration, his mouth working endlessly.

---

One day Mrs. Hazzard comes home from the hospital and sees her neighbour in the Hazzards' backyard, a widower named Conte McTavish. For thirty years this man and Mr. Hazzard carried on a silly feud, the origins of which they could not remember. When they retired they started to say good morning to each other and soon were talking in the driveway or over the hedge in a shy, embarrassed, happy way, like reunited friends. Mrs. Hazzard calls to him but he cannot hear her because he is swinging an axe. She makes her way slowly across the front lawn, past the house and into the back corner. The skies are heavy and the cold smell of snow is in the air. Her feet break through a granular crust to the powdery snow beneath, which is soft and dry and insulated from the winter by the brittle surface layer.

The snow is deep and some of it falls inside her boots. It makes her think of a day in her childhood when she was so angry with her mother that she walked through snow this deep to a park. There she sat on a swing anchored in a drift and cried and prayed that her mother would fall down dead. The force of this memory makes her stop in her tracks, dizzy with the power and malice of her childhood emotions. For a moment, the landscape tilts and spins. Then Conte appears again across the lawn, which is polished by the wind into sculpted waves, a white sea.

"Conte, what are you doing?" Mrs. Hazzard asks her neighbour.

He swings around, startled, a short heavy man with wire-rimmed glasses and a square red face. He says, "I couldn't sleep last night. I woke up thinking about the cherry tree. William and I were supposed to cut it down this fall. It's diseased. Don't you remember? I was going to help him, but then—" He looks down at the ground for a moment, shaking his head. "Tell him I've cut it down for him, would you? Tell him he doesn't have to worry about it any more."

Mrs. Hazzard does not say that Mr. Hazzard probably does not remember his neighbour or even know any more what a cherry tree is. Pale, meaty wood chips are scattered in a circle around them, like pieces of blasted flesh. The felled branches lie like charred limbs against the untouched snow. Mrs. Hazzard stares around at all of this in bewilderment and shock. She smells the sweet smell of the fresh wood. For a moment anger flares up in her like a flame in a lamp, protected from the winter wind. She is about to say to Conte: I wish you hadn't done this. I wish you'd let it stand. Perhaps it was not diseased at all but merely temporarily dormant. Perhaps it would have hung on much longer than you expected. You had no right. But when she opens her mouth to speak, Conte begins to weep, tears flowing easily down his vein-tracked cheeks. He stands with his hands, in thick stiff leather gloves, wrapped around the axe, sobbing like a boy, his breath coming out in white puffs of cloud.

"I'm just so sorry," he blubbers. "I'm so sorry about all those years we never spoke to each other. Such a loss. Such a stupid waste."

Mrs. Hazzard thinks about the sadness, the futility of everything. She thinks how ridiculous she and her neighbour are, two old people standing in the snow.

———————

The country doctor is transferring Mr. Hazzard to a rehab centre.

"Is this a step forward or a step back?" Mrs. Hazzard asks him.

He smiles at her gently, as though she is a child.

"Let's just think of it as a step," he says.

Always now, Mrs. Hazzard has the feeling that people are not telling her the truth. Or perhaps they are telling her the truth over and over in different ways but she cannot hear it. Mr. Hazzard grips the bed gate and shakes with tearless weeping.

"This may not be grief at all," the nurses tell Mrs. Hazzard. "It may be a nervous reflex, wires crossed somewhere."

Mrs. Hazzard does not believe this. "You are going to get better," she tells him. He looks up at her, his eyes so full of betrayal that she realizes now it is she who is telling the lies.

———————

Mrs. Hazzard is playing bridge. All afternoon she has listened to the *slap slap slap* of the cards falling on the table like waves lapping at a shore. She has played more brilliantly than ever before in her life but she has played blindly, like a person under hypnosis. She can scarcely remember a single hand. Today the cards seem to her mysterious and powerful. They have some message for her. The faces of the heavy-lidded queen, the unhappy king, the weak prince hold some complex secret. She stares at their gay geometric jackets in black, red and gold, at the stiff gestures of their tiny prophetic hands. As the cards spin into a soft pile, the red spots of the diamonds and hearts swim in her vision like drops of blood. Again and again today the ace of spades has turned up in Mrs. Hazzard's hand. What does this mean? She gazes at the spade and sees a gravedigger's shovel.

The women with whom she plays are bloated with widowhood. After their husbands died, they ate and ate until they swelled up like slugs, expanding to fill the void. She senses them waiting for her to join them in widowhood. These are her friends but today Mrs. Hazzard notices things about them: powder settling like sand in the creases of their faces, their bracelets jangling with potent charms, their pink hair, lipstick bleeding in rivers around their mouths.

"Mr. Hazzard has been transferred to White Oaks," she tells them.

"Oh, White Oaks," they say gravely. "Nobody ever comes out of there. How *is* Mr. Hazzard?" they ask.

She feels their eyes burning into her forehead. "He is thin," she tells them.

"How much longer?" they ask.

"How much longer for what?" she says.

A silence falls in the room. The women stare at Mrs. Hazzard, smug as fortune tellers behind cards fanned out in their hands. She can feel the force of their desire like something evil, a deadly spell. The room is hot and filled with their flowery perfume. Mrs. Hazzard cannot breathe. She rises suddenly, tipping the table. The cards slide sideways. The women's eyes grow wide with alarm. Mrs. Hazzard hurries down a hall to the bathroom, where she locks the door behind her. The women follow. They try the doorknob. They tap gently with their lacquered nails.

"Come out of there," they tell her. Mrs. Hazzard imagines them on the other side of the door, their soft bodies pressed together in the narrow hallway.

"I could not live without William," she tells them through the door. "If William dies, I will die."

"You will not be permitted to die," they tell her. "You will have to go on. There is nothing special about you. You will have to get through it just as we have. Then you will become one of us."

Outside it is cold. Dusk is falling. The snow on the ground is turning blue.

———————

It is nearly Christmas, and Mrs. Hazzard comes home and sees Conte McTavish's grandchildren building a snowman in front of his house. She stands on Conte's driveway and watches them, pleased to see something being created in this season of death. When she arrives the children have just mounted the head on the snowman. They add snow, packing it on where the spheres join. She watches them building up the body with handfuls, miracle of white flesh adhering to white flesh. It is a bright day. Mrs. Hazzard feels warmed by the life-giving sun. The snow is soft, the children's mittens stick to the snowman, pull off with difficulty. The snowman's curves are full and nourished, his belly swollen with health. He casts a robust shadow across the lawn.

Mrs. Hazzard stares at the children. They are amazing to her because they are so whole and lithe of limb, because they are so lucky, because they know little of their power to give life and to take it away. Above all, to take it away. The snowman belongs to the children, just as, in a way, Merilee holds the life of her father in her hands. It is within their means to create the snowman and to destroy him by their brief memories, their loss of faith, their susceptibility to distractions. The children inherit the earth.

"Hello," Mrs. Hazzard says, smiling at them.

"You are the woman whose husband is dying," they say.

"He is not dying," Mrs. Hazzard tells them. "He is only very ill."

The children stare at her. Their eyes grow wide, revealing the whites, so pure and unblemished, like the white of a hard-boiled egg, like snow before it has touched the ground. In their disbelief, the children are taking away with their hard-boiled eyes the life of my husband, Mrs. Hazzard thinks. The children's thick snowsuits distort their bodies, protecting them from the cold that Mrs. Hazzard feels and from something else within her, some fallacy.

The children go to the side of the house looking for branches piled there by Conte from the cherry tree. They bring out two vein-red sticks, which are multibranched, so that when they are stuck into the snowman's sides, they do not look like arms at all, but like whole circulatory systems.

"Do you have eyes for the snowman?" Mrs. Hazzard asks the children. She goes into her house and brings out a bowl of bright gumdrops she bought for Christmas though there is no one to eat them, she will have no visitors.

"I have brought you some eyes," she tells the children, holding out the bowl. The children look at the glittery orbs and begin to tremble. They run into the house, their scarves flying behind them like flags.

Dusk is falling. Lights come on up and down the street. Mrs. Hazzard stands in the snow with her bowl of candies, looking at the replete, sightless snowman.

———

Mrs. Hazzard has made for dinner a baked potato and a fried egg. This is a simple and healthy meal but she does not feel hungry. She is thinking about the pounds Mr. Hazzard has lost. Reaching for the telephone, she dials the long-distance number that will connect her with her daughter. The phone rings and rings. Finally Merilee answers breathlessly. She says she was on her way out, she was in fact in her car with the key in the ignition when she heard the phone ringing and came running back in. She thought it might have been someone important. Mrs. Hazzard looks out her kitchen window and tells Merilee that a heavy rain has been falling for several hours, though in Canada it should be snowing on the second day of January.

Merilee says, "God! I wish we had some of that where I am. The ground is cracking. We haven't had rain in three months. Water is rationed. What do you want, Mother? I'm late for my aerobics class."

Mrs. Hazzard tells Merilee that she has asked for an operation to put a tube in Mr. Hazzard's stomach because he cannot swallow food. Merilee is very angry.

"This is an artificial means to sustain him," she says. "We agreed not to do anything like this."

"I cannot sit here and watch him starve to death," says Mrs. Hazzard with emotion.

"Under the circumstances it would be the kindest thing," says Merilee. "You are doing this for yourself, not for him. You are being selfish."

"He's going to get better," Mrs. Hazzard insists.

"Oh, Mother," says Merilee bitterly, "you have always been so unrealistic."

"After the operation," says Mrs. Hazzard, "he's in God's hands."

Merilee snorts. "There must be somebody better than God we could put in charge of this," she says.

Mrs. Hazzard hangs up, quite shaken. She looks down at the potato and egg, solitary and undefiled on the plate. The egg yolk is the sun and Mrs. Hazzard will not break it, will not turn it into a watery eye. She puts the plate in the refrigerator.

She thinks about Merilee going out again to her car, walking across earth cracked like the surface of an overbaked cake. She pictures her at her aerobics class wearing one of those bright skin-tight costumes, and others in similar attire, young men and women leaning, bending trancelike before a wide mirror, stretching their firm, glistening, immortal limbs.

Dusk has fallen. Mrs. Hazzard goes out on to her porch with a bag of garbage. She sees the blind snowman, illuminated by Conte's porch light. The rain beats hard and steady on his shoulders, washing him away. It runs down his shrinking belly. His arms droop, loosened in their sockets. His flesh has become translucent as alabaster. It glows with a gentle but extraordinary quality, like a fading light bulb.

---

It is the morning of the operation and Mrs. Hazzard comes outside on her way to the hospital. She looks for the snowman in the neighbour's yard but he is gone. She stands on the white lawn, looking down at all that is left of him: the cherry tree branches lying on the ground.

At the hospital, a young intern intercepts Mrs. Hazzard on her way to Mr. Hazzard's room. He is tall and narrow-chested, with beautiful eyes and a woman's long lashes. Mrs. Hazzard does not know how such a thin, delicate man will be strong enough to save Mr. Hazzard.

"How is my husband?" she asks him. The intern tells her that Mr. Hazzard is dying. It is not the operation that is killing him, the intern explains, but pneumonia. He says pneumonia is something to be grateful for. It is known as the friend of the elderly. Mr. Hazzard will now die quickly. He will probably not live through the day.

"Death is very efficient," the intern says. "First the lungs shut down, then the kidneys, then the heart. *Bam bam bam*," he says, emphasizing his words by striking his fist in his hand. Mrs. Hazzard decides she does not like these young modern doctors. They are too smart, too confident, too unscathed.

A nurse indicates Mr. Hazzard's room. At first Mrs. Hazzard thinks they are playing a joke on her. You have shown me to the wrong room, she is going to say. This is not my husband. She is stunned by his appearance. He is unconscious and wearing an oxy-gen mask, through which Mrs. Hazzard can see his tongue rising and falling in his throat like a ship bobbing on a sea. Everything about his body now seems out of proportion. Parts of him have withered away and other parts look larger. His ears are like monarch butterflies, his nose is the size of a potato, his labourer's chest is mas-sive, heaving beneath his hospital gown. His hands have grown puffy, filling up with fluid like the balloon hands in a child's draw-ing. He looks, thinks Mrs. Hazzard, like a clown. It seems that he is mocking her, with this droll exterior, this transformation. You have left me, William, she thinks. You have turned into someone else.

Mrs. Hazzard thinks about her daughter. She feels Merilee will-ing Mr. Hazzard to die. Merilee has more power from a thousand miles away than Mrs. Hazzard has standing here, beside her hus-band's bed. How foolish I have been, she thinks. No one ever told her hope could be so cruel. Hope seems to be killing her now, at the same time that it is making it difficult for Mr. Hazzard to die. She thinks about calling the doctor back, calling Merilee, calling Conte McTavish. Yes, she would tell Conte. Yes, you were right. Better to cut the tree down than to hold out hope. "It's all right, William," she says to her husband now. "It's all right. You can let go. You can stop breathing." Suddenly, Mrs. Hazzard feels a tension flowing out of herself and the onset of a terrible, comforting fatigue.

———

Mrs. Hazzard walks in the dim yellow light of the hallways in her heavy zipped boots. Though people die here every day, every hour, the nurses, rushing past her, do not seem to grasp the magnitude of what is happening to her. She is filled up, Mrs. Hazzard is brimming with the knowledge of Mr. Hazzard's death. She is like a cup gently running over, yet there is no one to catch the precious overflow.

Now Mrs. Hazzard is down on the first floor looking for the

cafeteria, with her stiff square purse over her arm. She will buy a muffin. She must keep up her strength for the vigil. The big front doors swing open letting in warm air that sweeps around Mrs. Hazzard like a healing river. Hospital staff are coming in from the outdoors, coatless. They have been walking in the warm sunny streets carrying their winter coats over their arms here in January in the centre of the city in an old neighbourhood of sturdy brick homes. They are astounded, grateful, lightened by the springlike temperatures. It is my husband, Mrs. Hazzard wants to tell them. It is my husband who has brought this weather. He is dying and his body is absorbing all the cold.

*This book is set in Garamond, a standard
typeface used by book designers and printers
for four centuries, and one of the finest old styles
ever cut. Some characteristics of Garamond
to note are the small spur on the "G", the open
bowl on the "P", the curving tail on the "R",
and the short lower-case height and very
small counters of the "a" and "e".*